MURDER AT FIRST PITCH

The Ballpark Mysteries
Book 1

By

Nicole Asselin

pandamoon
publishing

www.pandamoonpublishing.com

Jacket design and illustrations © Pandamoon Publishing
Art Direction by Don Kramer: Pandamoon Publishing
Editing by Zara Kramer, Rachel Schoenbauer, Jessica Reino, and Ashley Hammond, Pandamoon Publishing

Pandamoon Publishing and the portrayal of a panda and a moon are registered trademarks of Pandamoon Publishing.

Library of Congress Cataloging-in-Publication Data is on file at the Library of Congress, Washington, DC

Edition: 1, version 1.00
ISBN 13: 978-1-950627-21-9

Dedication

For Grandma Asselin who loved a good mystery and Grandpa Asselin who loved the Red Sox.

MURDER AT FIRST PITCH

Chapter One

Crack.

The fastball careened off the splintered wooden bat and traveled into centerfield for a line drive single. The Abington Armadillos' first baseman rounded first and tried to stretch it into a double. Unfortunately, he wasn't as young as he once was and had lost his speed sometime during the presidential election of 2008. The second baseman received the ball and tagged the man legging it out well before he hit the bag. A groan went up from the players standing at the top of the dugout. Even though it was just a split squad scrimmage before the season started, the players took it very seriously.

Madeline Boucher leaned over the outfield railing. She breathed in the scent of the freshly cut grass at the Abington Armadillos ballpark. As she looked across the field at the player milling about, she felt that familiar tug of the game and her family's ballpark. It wasn't the easiest journey back home, but she felt that she was finally where she needed to be.

She took a quick glance down at her watch and let out a gasp. The time had gotten away from her and she now had to rush. Grabbing her bag, she dashed back to the stairs for the main concourse. She had to get ready for the new concessions party that night at the ballpark. It was her first night back full time with the team and she wanted to make sure she made a good impression. She knew most of the staff from family events, but she wasn't sure how they would react to her taking on a full-time position in the front office.

Madeline slammed into the front doors of the park and dashed towards the parking lot. She hopped into her car and quickly jammed the key into the ignition. As she pulled out of the parking lot, she thought back to a few weeks ago and how her life changed so quickly.

* * *

"Madeline, I'm sorry to tell you this, but we lost the contract." Her now ex-boss heaved a sigh and leaned back in her small office chair. "You know how hard it is here in Boston for this type of work. It's not like we have people beating down the door to hire writers for this type of technical writing. You'll have until the end of the month before the contract is completed."

Madeline weaved her way back to her desk through the cubicle farm of the small office. The rest of the cubes seemed quiet, and she had a feeling people were scrambling to apply for jobs as soon as they could. While she didn't love her job, it was a steady paycheck and kept her at least a bit independent from her family. She loved them dearly, but she was apprehensive about joining the family business.

Now there was no excuse. She knew what she had to do.

Madeline picked up the phone and dialed the front desk of the baseball park. She knew the number by heart from her daily conversations with her mom. After three quick rings, a woman with a strong Boston accent answered the phone. "Abington Ahmadillos Front Office, this is Eliza, how can I help ya?"

Madeline smiled into the phone. "Eliza, it's me, Maddie. Are my parents around?"

Eliza had been with the team for years and knew exactly what was going on at any moment through the ballpark. She even knew what the players were up to when they were out of the stadium. Her reach was everywhere. She was about Madeline's age, mid-thirties, but married with three kids. She was the standard "South Shore" women that most people knew about in the area. That meant she was obsessed with three things, her Ugg boots, her iced coffee from Dunks no matter the season, and her tanning. Madeline could hear her tapping her long fingernails against the desk as she was on the phone.

"Of course! Hey, before I send you over there, are you coming to the concession stand party next month? It's a big deal for the family and the park.... plus, you know what..." she paused dramatically. "Davis will be there."

Madeline smiled and took a deep breath at the mention of Davis. He was her former high school crush and now worked as the current security leader for the stadium. Six feet tall, dark hair, green eyes, and the body of a former baseball player, he was good looking, and Madeline also knew that he was a genuinely nice guy too. She hadn't heard any gossip about him recently, but they did see each other periodically at family game events. "Yeah, yeah, thanks Eliza for the heads up. I'll be there of course, but NOT to see Davis."

Eliza knew about Madeline's unrequited crush on Davis and laughed as she transferred the call to her mom's office phone. The phone rang once before Madeline's mom picked up.

"Marie Boucher, how can I help you?"

Madeline sighed in relief at hearing her mom's voice. "Bad news, Mom."

"Oh, sweetie, what's going on?"

"I lost my job. I have a month to find something new." Madeline choked up saying the words out loud. She held back her tears, took a deep breath, swallowed her pride, and asked the question that she had been waiting to do. "Mom, do you think there is a place for me with the team after all this? I just don't have the energy to do a long job search."

"Of course, that's great news! You know I've been trying to get you back here ever since you graduated college. Since it's the beginning of the season, it shouldn't be too hard to get you spun up on everything. Plus, you already have the background, and now I don't have to do any training with you. We need a new social media consultant, and I would love to fill it with my own beautiful daughter." Madeline's mother was the queen of the sale. She was the best advocate for the team, and she knew how to flatter and cajole her way into getting most things she wanted. As the saying goes, she could sell water to a fish.

* * *

Madeline stepped out of the shower as she thought about all the things that had changed in the last month. Her three cats wound their way around her legs and sat in the bathroom as she started to do her makeup and straightened her short brown bob.

While not the skinniest person out there, she wore her chubbiness as a point of pride. Once she turned thirty, it was so hard to keep the extra weight off, so she just decided to accept herself for who she was. And to be honest, she felt much better with a few more pounds on. She looked at herself in the mirror and fussed with the hem of her A-line bright emerald green dress. She had bought it in the team colors as a good introduction to the crew.

Her one-story cape style house was located in Abington, which was great for the new job. Even with a job in Boston at the time she bought the house, it was the cheapest option to live south of the city. So far it was just her and the three rescue cats, but it was home. It was nice to be so close to the family and the park, but still have her own place to get away from it all if needed.

Madeline pressed the automatic key to her Red Sox navy blue Honda Accord sitting in the driveway and hopped in. She took a deep breath and began the quick trip to the ballpark for the party. She pulled into the parking lot two minutes later and saw a crowd milling about the front entrance since the party hadn't started yet. She parked and waited a few minutes before spotting Eliza heading towards the office side entrance. She quickly turned the car off and sprinted over to Eliza, pressing the lock button as she did.

Shortly after the two women entered the office, the front doors were opened and the small, but excited crowd hustled in to get a load of the new options. The brand-new concessions area at the home of the Armadillos was sparkling and crowded with all sorts of local baseball bigwigs. Or at least people who thought they were bigwigs.

She spotted the owner of the Armadillos' fiercest rival, the Barnstable Barnstormers, hanging by the bar. It wasn't surprising since he was widely known for his alcoholic outbursts at games. "Eliza, is that William Chase over there by the bar?" Madeline tried to discreetly point over her shoulder to the offender. "I really hope we don't have to cut him off. My parents wouldn't want to make a scene."

Eliza rolled her eyes. "Billy is a lush. He just has to get his crap together and then he'll be fine." Madeline looked around to see if anyone was listening to their conversation.

"Shhhhh! I don't want my parents to hear me talking crap about a competitor. I don't know if I told you the good news. I'm coming back full time starting next week. The team needed someone to run their social media accounts, and I guess I'm cheap labor."

Eliza clasped her hands together and pulled Madeline into a big hug. She squeezed her tightly and squealed into her ear. "I'm so excited! We're going to have the best time working together. THE BEST!"

Madeline extracted herself from the hug and made a waving motion to the bar. Having been around the team since her grandfather had bought the team in the 80s, Madeline knew most of the people milling about the concessions stands. The family had decided to upgrade the concessions that year from the normal hot dog and burger stands to three more upscale options as well. They still had the burgers and dogs, but now there was a salad place, an ice cream joint, and a craft brewery area. While most people attended the Independent League for cheaper baseball, food was still important to keep them coming back for more.

The party was being held to let the season ticket holders and local dignitaries a chance to try the new options before opening to the general public. So far, it seemed to be a success. The line for the craft beer was stretched out into the party on the concourse itself. Madeline also spotted several old timers enjoying ice cream from a tiny replica baseball helmet. She smiled. Those were her favorites too. She used to attend Red Sox games with her grandfather and begged him to get the ice cream in the helmet every time they went. And every time he acquiesced.

As always, thinking of her Grandpa made her emotional. Even though the family had owned the team since before she was born, he was the one who instilled the love of the game and love of the Red Sox. He had passed away after she graduated college and she still missed him. It was hardest during the season, because she always wanted to discuss the latest team happenings. He was actually the one who got the family into the whole baseball racket in the first place. The team was having a downturn in the 1970s, brought on by bad professional baseball in the city. People just didn't want to go to any games. Her Grandpa bought the team in his own hometown for a pretty reasonable price when the town was trying to rehab its image and draw tourists in. The Abington Armadillos was one part of that.

She knew that people thought the name was weird. Armadillos weren't exactly native to New England. In fact, before the Red Sox won their first world series, the team was actually called the Huskies. Her Grandpa was such a fan of that 2004 team, he took the whole "Cowboy Up" theme coined by the players and thought about rebranding. At a Red Sox event that summer, one of the former players for that team, Kevin Millar, started expounding on the armadillos around his Texas homestead, and well, the name was changed. Alliteration is always a bonus when naming a sports team, and her Grandpa thought it had just enough tongue-in-cheek humor to make it work. And it did. The fans loved the change.

By the time Madeline was born in the 1980s, he had turned the team into a pretty lucrative business. While not affiliated with a specific pro team, the Armadillos even sent several players to the major leagues at some point. The lucky ones got sent to the minor leagues of the Red Sox in Maine and Rhode Island. Her Grandpa let her and her brother around the team as much as possible and they came to love them almost as much as the pros. Most of the kids in the area gravitated towards football and basketball, but not them. When her Grandpa passed away, Madeline's father took the helm of the team with her brother Ben as his deputy. He continued the family traditions of the park and even provided upgrades like Wi-Fi and table ordering in the stands. Her mother came aboard to run the front office, and everyone knew you had to go through her in order to get things done.

Now it was Madeline's turn to stake her claim with the team and her family. Madeline thought that losing her job had one silver lining, it might be fun working at the park again. She looked around the concourse again and noticed her brother deep in conversation with a man she'd never seen before. That was weird because she knew most of the people at the party, and this particular guy didn't seem to fit in. He was dressed for a night out in Boston, not a casual baseball opening party. He had on a three-piece black suit, black hair slicked back with gel, and dress loafers. About the same height as her brother, he seemed to be yelling something into her brother's face.

The man's face had turned an unbecoming shade of red as he continued yelling and pointed at her brother's chest. Ben held out his hands, as if he was trying to calm the man down. That just seemed to make the man angrier. Madeline noticed people around them started backing away and looking uncomfortable. She wondered if she should get security to head off any problems before it got too serious.

Ben looked over and caught her eye. She pointed at the guy talking to him and made a gesture asking who he was. He gave her a tiny shake of his head and turned back to the guy. The well-dressed man shoved a finger in her brother's face and stormed off. Madeline made her way over and grabbed Ben's arm, pulling him to a corner out of the way of the party.

"Who the heck was that? And why was he so angry?" She peppered him with questions as he rolled his eyes. He hated questions. They were relatively close as siblings, only separated by two years, but got on each other's nerves very easily.

He had one more eye roll and waved a dismissive hand. "Maddie, don't worry about it. It's just some guy I had a disagreement with a few days ago. He was talking crap about our new catching prospect and I disagreed with his opinion. Nothing more. He's just a guy with a vested interest in baseball." He paused and looked around. "Shouldn't you be mingling with your new co-workers instead of interrogating me?"

With that, he turned on his heel and headed back towards the craft beer stand. She stood there thinking about what he had said. She didn't know if she believed him. What does a "vested interest" in baseball even mean? A fan? A player? An agent? That guy looked way too angry to be concerned about some catcher on an independent league baseball team. Why would Ben lie to her though? She hoped he wasn't in trouble, but there was nothing she could do about it now. As she turned back to the crowd, she spotted Davis making his way towards her.

She glanced around anxiously looking for Eliza to be her wingwoman in this conversation, but she was nowhere to be found. She took a deep cleansing breath and turned back in his direction. No time for awkwardness. She straightened her shoulders and gave Davis a big smile as he arrived at her side.

Chapter Two

Madeline had to remind herself not to stare at him, but to use her words and converse with him. Mental pep-talks always helped her in situations like these. She was helplessly awkward sometimes around the guys she tended to crush on. He was just so dreamy. She remembered taking the time during college to follow along with his baseball career. He never made it very far but played for a lot of independent teams before blowing out his knee in a playoff game. Being a local, he knew about her family's team and her family was only too happy to bring on a baseball player to the crew.

"Hey, man," she cringed internally at her word choice and tried to mask her discomfort with a big smile. "How's it going, Davis?"

He gave her a brief smile. "Hey, Maddie, welcome back. I heard you're going to be around a lot now, that's going to be great. I hate to be quick about this, but do you know the guy who your brother was just talking to?

Madeline started. Davis was watching that whole thing? Why did he seem so concerned?

"No, he told me it was some guy he met while discussing baseball or something. He was kind of cagey about it." She shrugged to shake off her unease. She didn't want Davis to think she was being a worrywart or imagining problems that weren't there. It was probably nothing anyway.

"Hm," he said, scratching his freshly shaved chin. "He didn't look familiar, and I got a weird vibe from him. Let me know if you hear anything else." He turned and threaded his way through the partygoers towards to the offices at the front of the stadium.

Davis was usually much friendlier than that. He must have really been worried about that guy. Well, Madeline thought, she hoped the trouble was over for the night. Her friends came running over with a cheap plastic cup of white wine, her favorite. The quizzing over Davis started immediately and Madeline decided to just let it go and focus on getting the season started.

* * *

The rest of the days leading up to Opening Day passed by in a blur. The party was scheduled two weeks before the actual game day, and the rest of the time was spent checking with season ticket holders and making sure the ballpark was ready for guests. As the social media consultant, Madeline was putting the word out everywhere. With only a week left to get everything handled, she and the family were putting extra hours in the ballpark and the community to ramp up interest. Luckily, the team was seeing a spike in season ticket sales, probably because they were so much cheaper than heading into town for a Red Sox game. Plus, the team was a family fun escape for the community. The new concessions were just one part of the Opening Day plan. The team also added a kid's area where the mascot would hang out between innings, a few interactive pitching and hitting areas, and contests to run during the game that would make people more eager to come out to the ballpark.

Madeline felt she had settled in quite nicely and decided to take a stroll around the ballpark just to check things out. With the big day fast approaching, she wanted to get one last feel of the place while it was empty. She headed out of the office at the front of the stadium and walked through one of the tunnels to the seats behind home plate. The grounds crew was out doing some final touches on the infield dirt and pitcher's mound. On the first base side, one of the coaches was playing long toss with the newest pitcher, and out in right field were about ten players going through morning stretches.

As she continued down the field, she scanned the dugouts out of habit looking for favorite players. Before she turned back to the outfield, something glinted in the corner of her eye from inside the visitors' dugout. It was a quick flash of light, as if bouncing off something metal on the dugout floor. She tried signaling someone, but everyone was too busy with their daily routines. Dave, the head groundskeeper, was at the pitcher's mound raking the dirt. He'd been with the family for years and was a stadium staple. He was engrossed in his task so Madeline decided to check things out for herself.

She turned and made her way to the dugout, knowing she saw something in there. No one was supposed to be around the visitor's side of the ballpark today as far as she knew. The visiting team wouldn't show up for three more days at least. She made her way over and slowly walked down the two steps into the visiting bench area.

The floor was cement covered with a fine layer of dirt, which made her wonder if the grounds crew had a chance to clean the dugout yet. As she made her way down the bench, an overwhelming smell assaulted her nose causing her to choke. It smelled like a dead animal, and she hoped that it wasn't. It would not be good to have to clean up roadkill in the dugout. She covered her nose with her hand and got closer to the doorway of the visitors' dugout at the end of the bench. Her eyes watering, she looked into the doorway of the clubhouse and screamed.

There, sprawled on the ground of the dugout was the guy that her brother had been fighting with the other night. Blood pooled around his head and his eyes stared straight up at her and she slowly backed away from the body. She still didn't know his name. That was the first thing she thought about. Next to his body was a bat caked in blood laid on the dugout floor. She felt sick to her stomach and hurried to the steps of the dugout.

At her scream, Dave had run over and met her at the top of the stairs. "Maddie, is everything okay? I heard you scream."

She pointed a trembling finger towards the back of the dugout at the man laid across the ground.

"Oh crap, is he dead?" Dave swept the hat off his head with a worried expression.

She nodded and took a few steps onto the field. Anything to get away from the gruesome sight. She had read enough mysteries and saw enough TV to know that she shouldn't touch or move anything, and she knew she had to get out of that space before she embarrassed herself by getting sick.

Dave followed her to the dirt surrounding the infield and put a hand on her shoulder. She took some deep breaths and tried to steady herself. She knew it wouldn't do any good to breakdown or freak out. She could do that later.

She turned to Dave. "Do you have your phone? Call 911. I'm going to get Davis down here to secure everything. We can't have people walking around willy-nilly with…well, you know." She waved her hand toward the dugout. He nodded and pulled his phone out of his back pocket and began to dial. Madeline walked towards the front of the field where she could access the offices.

She ran to the first door she saw and leaned against the wall inside. She took some more deep breaths, shook herself, and began the walk to the offices down the hallway. Her parents weren't in yet, which she was grateful for, she didn't want to have to break the news to them right away. She needed to think. Davis, on the other hand, was always the first one in and last one out, so she knew he'd be in his office.

She tapped on the inside of the open-door frame and leaned her head in. "Davis, we have a problem." She continued into his office and sat in the guest chair across his desk.

He looked up at her from behind his laptop workstation. As security lead he had monitors set up on one corner of the desk and assorted radios plugged into outlets along the wall. "I heard. Dave radioed me right after he called the police. Are you okay?" He looked at her intently with his hands folded. She squirmed under his intense gaze.

"I'm fine. I mean, it's a little weird finding a dead body. Especially a dead body of someone I just saw alive and well recently. I mean, I've read a ton of books with dead people in them, but seeing one in the flesh? That's a whole other deal." She could still see the guy's eyes staring into nothing. She shivered again. Suddenly she jumped up. "Has anyone called my parents? If Dave radioed you, did you call my dad? It's still early, but they must be on their way here now."

Davis' phone gave off a shrill beep. He glanced down at the text and sighed. "Police are here. I think I saw your dad come in a few minutes ago. We're going to need to get the family together later today to think of a plan for after this incident. Go grab your dad and meet me down at the field so you can meet with the officers. They're going to need to take your statement." He grabbed his light jacket off the back of his seat and took off out of the office.

Madeline took a minute to collect herself before following him out the door and walking down the short hallway to her father's office. The door was open and the lights were on. She saw her father looking at some papers and writing notes in the small notebook he always carried with him.

At her knock, her father looked up and put the papers to the side. "Maddie! I just heard the news. Dave radioed the entire staff to let them know what happened. Are you okay? Do you know who the guy was?" He got up from his desk and took her into a big hug. She couldn't believe word got around so fast. Dave was really on top of things this morning.

"I spoke with your Mom and Ben; they are both coming in early now. Let's get down to the field and get Davis. Hopefully it was a tragic accident and we can move on quickly and get ready for Opening Day."

Madeline followed him out the double doors to the field level. She had only been gone for ten minutes, and there were already a bunch of uniformed cops and two plainclothes guys clustered around the visitor's side of the field. From her many years of watching "Law & Order" reruns, she felt she could reasonably determine that the two guys not in uniforms were the detectives. Davis stood talking to one of the men at the top of the dugout stairs. He waved them over.

"Robert, Maddie, this is Detective Stevenson. He's in charge of the investigation." Davis introduced the two to the tall man standing next to him. He clearly looked like a detective with a face that said he took no nonsense, dark hair, dark eyes, and a trench coat. It looked like he stepped out of a twenties gangster movie. So, it was a bit chilly out, being April in New England, but a trench coat seemed out of place.

"Mr. Boucher, it's nice to meet you both. As Davis said, I'll be heading up the investigation from here on in. The Abington PD will coordinate things here locally, and the DA's office will handle part of the investigation in conjunction with the local PD and state police. We're looking at it as a potential homicide for now. Madeline, you're the one who found the body, correct?"

She nodded.

"Did you recognize him at all? Do you know who he is?" The detective peered at Madeline, hand poised over his notebook.

She shook her head. "I don't know him by name. He was at the party we had the other night, but we weren't introduced."

The detective nodded and motioned for her to wait. He led her father to the dugout steps to presumably see if he knew the victim. Davis grabbed her elbow and pulled her off to the side.

"Maddie, we need to talk about your brother. It turns out the guy was killed with the bat found in the dugout. No one had officially confirmed it yet, but it seems the most likely conclusion. There was a bunch of bats in the cubby of the dugout, so I'm going to assume that is where the weapon came from for now. Not many people have access to that area outside of the security team and front office when no visitors are in the stadium. It's not going to be good for your brother that he was seen fighting with the victim so soon before the murder. And of course, he has access to the park. Still no word on the guy's name?" Davis looked at her.

Madeline shook her head trying to think back to if she ever heard the guy's name before. "No, I haven't talked to Ben about what happened since that night. He's on his way now though; hopefully we can get some answers."

She stopped talking as the paramedics placed the body bag on the stretcher and leveraged it out of the dugout. She shivered again even though the day was starting to warm up. It was one thing to see all this action on TV and quite another to see it in person. The police had set up crime scene tape and she noticed that they had started dusting the dugout for fingerprints. The fine dust hung in the still air and Madeline wondered if it would do much good. There had been people in and out of the dugout for the week leading up to the game for practice and whatnot.

Detective Stevenson and her father walked out of the dugout towards the edge of the dugout closest to home plate. Another officer came over to where Davis and Madeline were standing. "You two don't need to stay here, just don't leave the park. The detective is going to have to question everyone who was here this morning, and I know that since you found the body, he'll be coming to see you first."

She nodded at the officer and asked if she could wait in her office. The young officer didn't look much older than some of the interns the family had working in the office during their summer breaks.

He made sure to remind Madeline again not to leave the park and Madeline made sure Davis knew that she was heading back to the office. She felt a little shaky from the experience; seeing dead bodies was not normal. Her heart was beating faster, and she shuddered at the images stuck in her head. She tried taking a deep calming breath. As she turned back towards the concourse, Davis stopped her with a hand on her shoulder.

"If you need anything, Maddie, let me know. I'm always around if you need to talk about what happened today." His eyes showed his concern. Before she could respond, the detective waved him over to where he was discussing things with her father.

She trudged to the front office. She couldn't decide if what she saw was concern as a friend or something more. Maybe it's because she was the boss' daughter, and maybe he was just trying to do a full-service job. He was just so cute. She wanted to read more into his concern. Nothing like a dead body to bring two people closer together.

Chapter Three

Madeline thought the hours seemed to stretch along forever. Finally, two detectives appeared at her office for her official statement. They had spent the majority of the morning at the crime scene. She shuddered as she thought of how the dugout was now tainted by the crime. If the team kept it pretty low-key, hopefully the other teams wouldn't get superstitious and not want to play here. That would be a disaster for the league and the team. Not to mention the pain to her parents and her new job. Baseball was an extremely superstitious sport, and they definitely didn't need to project a bad-luck image to the players. Just ask the Red Sox and the "Curse of the Bambino" or the Cubs and the "Billy Goat Curse."

After introducing his partner, Detective Jefferson, Stephenson sat down and began to ask Madeline about the events leading up to her finding the dead body. The two detectives looked at her closely with pens hovering over their notebooks. Just like old school detectives, they didn't seem to know that someone could use technology to take better notes. Madeline felt uncomfortable, almost as if they were treating her as a suspect. She felt a drop of sweat bead at the bottom of her back, which could have been just the heat of her un-airconditioned office or a bit of nervousness. Her office let in a ton of sunlight, and when it was as clear as it was out, her office heated up quickly. She hoped that was the reason. Not some sort of panic attack.

She retold them about her walk to the field on most mornings, how she saw Dave and the grounds crew, and then how she noticed the flash of light from the visitors' dugout. As she looked back, she realized that it was probably from his watch or something glinting in the morning sunlight. She once again pictured the body, his unseeing eyes, and the pool of blood behind his head. She shuddered.

"Do you recall seeing the man enter the stadium in the morning?" Detective Jefferson asked while looking down at his notebook. She thought back to when she arrived at the stadium early in the morning. She didn't remember seeing any cars out of the ordinary in the parking lot. She remembered parking, putting her keys and purse in her office before walking down to the field. She saw only a few other people in the office and concourse, but she knew all those people.

"Nope. The only people I saw were other employees of the ballpark. I only saw that guy once before, at the concession party the other night, like I told you. I never saw him before that." She watched as the detectives scribbled in their notebooks. She wondered what they were writing, it didn't seem like she said all that much. "Did you identify the guy yet?"

Detective Stephenson looked over at his partner and then back to her. "Does the name Christopher Dailey mean anything to you?" He leaned forward expectantly, as if she could break the case wide open right then and there.

She thought back through her mental rolodex of names. "No…I don't think so. Should it?" She was usually good with names, but this name didn't seem to register.

He sighed and leaned back into the chair, rubbing his neck. "It's the victim. He is a local baseball scout, but that's all we could find out so far. He had an ID with him in his wallet. I thought since you were part of the front office you would know him."

"Well, seeing as it has only been a few weeks since I started here, I don't know that I would be able to name everyone working here. Plus, he's a scout. That's not really someone affiliated with the team. I mean, he's considered an independent contractor I would think. You'd have to talk to my mom. She has all the human resource files on any employees and contractors. As I said, I saw him once before today, and now you just told me who he was."

"Well, we're going to be investigating here for a little while, so we'd appreciate it if you didn't leave the area or talk to anyone else about this while the investigation is ongoing. Can you do that?" The detective looked at her with a hard stare.

She nodded her head, and at that the two detectives shut their notebooks, thanked her for her time, and walked slowly out of her office. It was then she noticed Davis standing outside the door. He ushered the two men down the hall to her father's office. Madeline peeked around the corner of the doorframe and caught a quick glimpse of the back of her brother's head as the door shut behind the two detectives.

Madeline hustled back behind her desk and flipped open her laptop screen. "Christopher Dailey," she said to herself out loud. "What is your story?" She fired up the search engine on her computer and typed his name in. The first couple of stories that popped up were definitely not about the guy from the dugout. They were mostly about some guy in Florida that died in a canoe accident. She scrolled quickly past those links. About halfway down the page she found an entry for Chris Dailey on a local newspaper site. She clicked on the article and drummed her fingers on the desk while it loaded. When an image popped up on her screen, she gasped.

It was a mugshot of the victim! How did her brother know someone that had a mugshot?

She quickly scanned through the article and found out that Chris Dailey was busted for running an illegal betting ring out of his house on the North Shore of Boston. He had spent five years in prison before getting released for good behavior. After that, he seemed to drop off the face of the earth. She kept searching, but only found a couple of social media sites with his name that she would check later.

She stretched her arms behind her head and tried to wrap her brain around the events of the day. A rumble from her stomach reminded her that she hadn't eaten since early that morning and it was now lunchtime. She grabbed her purse and ran down the hallway to the front desk. Eliza was there standing (or sitting) guard near her mom's office door.

Eliza jumped up as soon as she saw Madeline approach. "Maddie! What the heck!? Why didn't you call me when you found the dead guy?" Madeline shushed her with her hands and rolled her eyes.

"They told me not to talk to anyone." Madeline rolled her eyes. "Anyway, are you in for lunch?" Eliza saw Madeline had her purse and grabbed hers as well. They walked out into the ballpark concourse and headed toward the only open food option during the off season.

Centerfields was located, as the name suggested, in the outfield of the park, just outside the stadium gates. A person could enter the sports bar from either side of the park, and the owners had been family friends for years. They provided great entertainment in the off season, and the rent they paid to the stadium helped the family keep the place afloat in the lean times. Plus, it was the perfect place for a quick lunch when working at the ballpark on a non-game day.

Eliza and Madeline were creatures of habit. They went to their usual booth overlooking the parking lot and ordered their usual meal of cheeseburgers, fries, and diet cokes. They didn't have to place their orders anymore. Their waitress, Veronica, knew them and put the orders in before they could even sit down. After she placed the two drinks on the table and walked away, Madeline looked around to make sure no one could overhear her.

"Eliza, did you know a Chris Dailey?" If anyone would know who he was, it would be Eliza. Not only the receptionist at the ballpark, she had a way with names and faces that bordered on scary. If a person came to the park once, she'd remember them forever.

"Why? Is that the name of the dead guy?" At Madeline's nod, Eliza scrunched up her face as if thinking back through her catalog of faces. "Wait! That name does sound familiar. He came in to talk to your brother a few weeks ago about a prospective scouting venture. It was before you started. It was about some college player, I think. He was only around for like fifteen minutes before he stormed out of the office. He didn't seem too pleased at whatever your brother had to say to him. The guy was sketchy to the extreme, too. Didn't look like a scout. More like a sleazy guy from a bar or someone who would be on the ponies or something." She made a gagging motion. "I was definitely not a fan."

Madeline sat back in the booth as her burger arrived at that moment. After the chaos of the morning, she knew she should eat. She had to keep her strength up to get through this mess.

Madeline realized her initial impression of the dude wasn't that far off. She combined her impression with what she found online about his criminal history and knew he wasn't the type of guy her brother should or would be associating with on the regular. She would have to get with Ben later that night to figure out the real story.

She tried changing the subject with Eliza and soon they were gossiping about other people they knew. Anything to take their minds of the murder for a few minutes. Eliza was always entertaining and had Madeline laughing at her observations in no time. It helped alleviate her stress immediately. Of course, she knew that the stress would come right back when they stepped back in the office.

After lunch, they parted ways at her desk and Madeline continued down the hallway to her office. Lunch had only taken an hour, and it looked like the detectives were still shut in her dad's office talking to Ben. She casually slowed down before getting to her door when she saw her dad's door swing open.

The two detectives were on either side of her brother and appeared to be walking him towards the front entrance. He caught her eye and gave her a quick, tenuous smile.

He tried to reassure her as he walked by. "Maddie, I have to go down to the station for some more questions. Can you get the paperwork in order for next week's game?" Ben wasn't handcuffed, but the detective flanking him on either side seemed serious. At her shocked expression, he smiled again, "Don't worry about it. I'll be back to work tomorrow morning."

At that, the trio headed down the hall to the front gates of the ballpark. She wondered if he was being arrested. Since she didn't see any handcuffs, she hoped it was a good sign. Hopefully they just wanted to ask him some questions. She turned as she heard her dad approach.

"Dad, what's going on? Do we need to close the offices for the rest of the day? What do the police need?" Madeline peppered her dad with as many questions as she could think of. She didn't notice Davis was in the hallway until he spoke up.

"I spoke with Detective Stephenson before they came in here, and he did mention that your brother is a suspect. They wanted him to go down for questioning, and of course, he's cooperating. They haven't arrested him yet, which is a good thing. The lawyer is meeting him at the police station so he should be covered. Chris Dailey was apparently a bad guy so it won't be hard to find more suspects I would think. Your brother just told the police that the two men had a falling out over a baseball prospect deal." Davis ran a hand through his hair. "For now, we'll just act as business as usual. The crime scene people are finishing up on the field and the team should be able to resume access to it tomorrow. But I would recommend the team practice somewhere else for a few days. Is there anywhere else the team can go for practice while we figure things out?" He addressed that final question to her father, who stroked his graying beard in thought.

"I think so. There is a practice field down the street. Nothing fancy, but I'll talk to Billy this afternoon before the bus gets here to work out the logistics. I'm sure the players will understand." The team provided players with a shuttle bus from the local T stops and commuter rails, so they didn't have to drive to every practice. A majority used public transportation, and this just provided them a way to get to the ballpark quickly from the subway stops.

Madeline whipped out a notebook to take a few quick notes on the updated plans. Her father looked at her before turning back into his office. "Maddie, work on getting some sort of family statement together just in case the press start calling. And make sure you get the website announcement about the Opening Day ticket giveaway up and running. I know you were working on it before everything happened."

Of course, he was thinking about the team. With Opening Day so close, the family couldn't let a little thing like murder derail the plans for the beginning of the season. She walked back to her desk with a million thoughts in her head about the murder. It's not that she didn't trust the police, but she thought she could maybe move things a little quicker by finding out more about the victim. Her brother couldn't have been the only person to get in a fight with this guy. She settled back behind her laptop and wiggled the mouse. The page on her screen was on the article about Chris Dailey's arrest. Starting tomorrow, she was going to find out everything she needed to know about that guy.

Chapter Four

The next day, Madeline woke up after a restless sleep. Seeing dead bodies is not something that helps ease a person into peaceful dreamland, that's for sure. She stretched, reaching her arms behind her head and grabbed her phone. She found about ten text messages from Davis asking her to get to the stadium as soon as possible. All sent before 8:00 a.m., so it must've been serious. She quickly hopped into the shower, pulled her hair back into a headband, and dashed to her car.

One benefit from losing her job in the city was the new lack of a commute. Her house was in the town she grew up in and the ballpark was only a five-minute drive away. On nice days, she could even walk to the park if she wanted to, which she rarely did. Exercise was not her favorite activity in the world, so driving it was.

Her parents also ended up building a house near the park which was why they had such easy access to the ballpark as needed. Madeline and her brother grew up near the park and even when she got her job in the city, she bought a house close to the family.

Madeline pulled into a parking space close to the front entrance of the ballpark. She was surprised to see a television van out front. She knew it was a story, but the news seemed to be excessive. She thought at most it would be a newspaper or blog story. It didn't look like they were filming at that very moment, so Madeline hoped she could rush in without anyone seeing her. She pulled the hood of her sweatshirt over her face, took a hold of her purse and jumped out of the car. She walked as quickly as she could to the front door and was almost there when she heard her name being yelled across the parking lot.

"Madeline Boucher! It's me, Jennifer Roberts! From high school! Remember!?" A tall, leggy blonde made her way over to Madeline from the news van carrying a microphone, followed by a chubby cameraman in a stained Red Sox T-shirt.

Madeline tried to get into the door pretending she didn't hear the woman yelling her name. She shook the door, but it was locked and she couldn't get her keys out of her purse in time. Of course. She plastered a smile on her face and turned around.

"Jennifer, so good to see you." She cringed at the fake sound of her own voice. This whole thing was not going to be pleasant. "What can I help you with today? Are you here about the exciting plans we have for Opening Day next week?" Madeline smiled, knowing how much she was probably annoying the reporter.

Her camera guy turned towards Madeline even though she still had her hood pulled up over her face. Jennifer shoved the microphone dangerously close to Madeline's face. "Do you or the Boucher family have any comment regarding the allegations of murder against the prodigal son, Benjamin Boucher?"

Madeline looked shocked and Jennifer repeated the same question twice.

Finally, Madeline blurted out, "No comment!" and turned away from the camera. She heard the door rattle behind her, and an arm reached out and pulled her inside the gates. She found Davis there with a grim look on his face. Jennifer Roberts was still outside yelling questions as he relocked it and led her to the office conference rooms.

"Davis, what's going on? I thought everything was going to be taken care of yesterday. Why would she need or want a comment from me?" Madeline followed him into the conference room and looked at the assembled group. The whole family was there, minus Ben. Her mother was standing at the window with a wad of tissues in her hand. She was ripping them into tiny pieces as she stared out the window. Her father was at the head of the table with his hands forming a steeple in front of him. The rest of the table included Eliza, Davis, a few managers of the office, and Billy, the team manager.

"Maddie, please take a seat. We have some things to discuss today." Her father gestured to the chair next to him. She sat down heavily still wondering what was happening. Why wasn't Ben there?

"As you all know, there was a tragic incident here yesterday at the ballpark. A man was found dead in the visitors' dugout. After investigating most of the day and night, the police department has ordered us to wait a day or two before opening the visitors' dugout to players and personnel. They want to make sure they can officially clear the scene first." He rubbed his hands across his face. "Davis, as security lead, you'll be the point person with the police. They don't believe the investigation will impede the schedule of Opening Day events we have, but that's subject to change obviously. I'm going to hand over the rest of the meeting to you to discuss the rest of the security issues."

Her father yielded the floor to Davis, who moved to stand in front of the room. "I know this is a hard time right now, but the police have assured me that they would do their best to make sure this investigation would go as smoothly as possible. I know you're wondering where Ben is this morning. Well, he's an official person of interest in the investigation, so we have decided to have him stay away from the ballpark for the time being."

Madeline gasped at the last part of Davis' speech. Her brother? A suspect in a murder? What in the heck was the world coming to? "There is no way Ben killed anyone. The police are looking in the wrong direction!" She jumped out of her seat and looked at Davis.

Warily, he looked at her and gestured her to sit down. "Maddie, we all know he didn't do anything wrong, but for now it's just easier to control the media and the investigation if he stays away from the ballpark. That way there is no semblance of conflict of interest, plus it will ease the distraction leading up to Opening Day. I don't need to remind you that there will be some media here that day, and if we can keep the spotlight off the murder as much as possible, we have a chance to get out of this situation with very minimal damage."

Her mom chimed in. "In regards to press, a simple 'no comment' should suffice. We're crafting a statement now that will be released in the next few hours which will be the brunt of our comments on this horrible situation."

At that, both of her parents got up and left the conference room. As she watched them head down the hallway to her father's office, she sat in her seat for a few minutes longer, thinking about how everything changed since yesterday afternoon. She knew her brother couldn't have murdered that guy, even if he was seen fighting with him. Plus, there would be no way her brother would get up that early in the morning to attack that man. If she got to the park around eight in the morning and spotted the victim at eight-thirty, it was way too early. Her brother didn't usually make it into the ballpark until ten at the earliest. Dailey didn't look like he'd been dead that long, so she just didn't believe that her brother could do it. She felt confident in her timeline, even if most of her knowledge came from mystery novels.

She made her way to the office to craft up a statement for her parents to read regarding the murder and investigation. She typed it up, printed it out, and took another look to make sure it sounded good and professional. She hoped it would head off any more questions for the time being.

FOR IMMEDIATE RELEASE

It is with great sadness that the Abington Armadillos would like to announce there was a tragic incident here at the field that involved one person being killed. The police are investigating this event and will provide any other available details. The Boucher family and the team would like to extend our deepest condolences to the family of the victim and will continue to cooperate with the police in any capacity they deem necessary. Please contact the Abington Police Department with any other questions or queries at this time.

After attaching the release to an email and sending it over to her mother for dissemination, she leaned back in her chair. She reached into her office mini-fridge, one of the perks of working in her own office and pulled out a Diet Coke. Now that she had time to herself, she wanted to continue to learn more about the victim. At least she wanted to try and figure out who wanted him dead because she refused to believe her brother was guilty of this crime. She fired up her laptop and typed Christopher Dailey's name into the search bar. She skipped over the article about his jail stint since she already looked at that. She found his social media pages and clicked on those. If there is one way to get to know a person, it's through their social media presence.

"Ah-ha!" His Facebook page wasn't private, so she could access anything he posted and anything anyone else posted on his page. She knew this would help her find some people who might have had it in for him. Shoot, even she didn't know him, but she knew that she didn't like him. She scrolled down through his postings to see if anything jumped out at her. About halfway through the page of mostly sports memes, she hit the jackpot. "Bingo!" she said out loud to her empty office.

Some woman named Claire Fraser had posted an angry screed about how Christopher had cheated her and her family out of money by promising their son a baseball career. He apparently took their money over six months ago and hadn't delivered on any of his baseball promises since. Her son ended up depressed and hooked on drugs. The woman was convinced it was all Dailey's fault.

Madeline thought that sounded interesting. So not only was he a bookie, he was a scammer of potential baseball players as well. She wondered if that was part of the connection with her brother.

While she ruminated on that, she peered at her desk calendar and realized she hadn't finished some of her real tasks for Opening Day which was now five days away. She still had to get the word out and start some giveaways with the local radio stations. She knew that so far they had planned an Opening Day carnival with games and food, but she wasn't sure how ticket sales were doing with all the drama going on. She decided to head down to her mother's office to get a proper count. Her investigation into Christopher Dailey's life would have to wait until another day.

Chapter Five

The rest of the week leading up to the Opening Day game passed by in a blur. Between getting the promotions out for upcoming games and fending off press, Madeline didn't seem to have a lot of time to do any investigating on her own. The police had finally cleared the ballpark as a crime scene, so the team returned to the home field the day before the start of the season. Billy, the manager, decided to have a full day's practice the day before the game since that was the first time they had been on the home field in a while.

Madeline took her computer out to the right field seats to work on one of the picnic tables in the outfield while the team practiced. The crack of the bat was just what she needed to get her mind in gear. The game was already sold out for Opening Day, which was good news. The Boston Red Sox also agreed to run a promotion with the team to give away free Sox tickets at team events during the season, the first event being the season ticket holder gala the weekend after the opening game. Even for a minor league team, they had a dedicated group of people who bought season tickets every year. Throughout the year, the team loved to hold a few events during the season to thank those ticket holders for their patronage.

She was in the midst of pulling together a list of attendees for the gala and trying to decide what to include in the "swag bag" when she heard two people arguing from the behind the right field wall. Not one to let a potential drama-filled moment pass, she eased her way closer to the wall to see if she could hear better what was going on. Beyond the right field was a park area where people could congregate before and after the games if they wanted to. At that moment, two men were standing there talking in heated tones and pointing at each other.

Madeline recognized one of the guys as a scout for the team that her brother had pointed out before. A well-respected local guy, he supported local athletes more than anyone else according to her brother. Tall, with fair hair and an athlete's build, this guy was one of the good ones. She thought she remembered being introduced to him as Tom. The guy he was arguing with on the other hand didn't look at all familiar to her. He was a bigger guy, with a "dad bod" type of physique: a little round in the middle. He had on a baseball hat and was jabbing his finger into Tom's chest.

"You need to fix this, Tom. We had a deal. I don't care if Chris is dead. My son will play for the team if it's the last thing I do." With one last jab at Tom's chest, the other guy turned and started to walk back towards the parking lot.

"Rich, you need to calm down. Call my office and we'll talk about this later," Tom said to the man's retreating back. Shaking his head, he walked off in the opposite direction of the parking lot into one of the side entrances to the ballpark.

Madeline sat back at the table with her chin resting on her hand. That was interesting, she thought. While she was lost in thought, she didn't notice a person sit down across from her.

"Hey, Maddie, how's it going?" Davis waved a hand in front of her face. "All set for tomorrow's game?"

She thought he looked more tired than usual and put it down to probably not getting much sleep while working with the police on this whole thing. She wondered if he ever thought of joining the Abington Police after his baseball career was over. Was he really happy just being the head of security for a local baseball team?

"We're ready for Opening Day, as you can see." She swept her arm out across the field. "The team is looking good, and I have all the social media sites primed and ready for a storm of action tomorrow. Any updates on the case?" She leaned forward expectantly. Depending on what he told her now, she would decide if she should let him know about the two pieces of information she had learned that day.

He sighed. "Still no leads as of yet. Your brother turned out to have a pretty solid alibi for the time of the murder, which I guess was about five in the morning the day you found the body. They are now questioning everyone again who had access to the park at that time in the morning to see what they can find out. They're coming by this afternoon to do some more interviews. Will you be around?'

"Of course!" Madeline said. "Anything to make sure they find the crazy person who did this. Speaking of crazy people, do you know if the police looked into his social media? I found some pages this week and definitely think there are a few people who were angry with Chris Dailey. Any one of them could be his killer!" Madeline continued on, even though Davis was staring at her with wide eyes and his mouth agape. "And just a minute ago, like right before you came out here, there was this guy talking to Tom, the scout, about some secret deal he had going on with Chris. He mentioned his name and that he was dead! How many other dead guys named Chris could he know?" She leaned forward excitedly, hoping Davis would see the value to her snooping. Instead, he leaned back and shook his head.

"Maddie, you have to let the police do their jobs. You running around thinking you're investigating things only wastes your own time. I'm working with the police now, and they told me they have several leads. I believe them. Maybe you should, too." Davis got up from the table. "Plus, we have enough to worry about with the start of the season. Let's just get through the next couple of days, okay?"

She nodded. As he turned to leave, she made a face at his back and gave him a mock salute. "Sir, yes, sir."

He turned around, caught her face, gave a quick smile, and rolled his eyes. "I know you're trying to be funny, but please just be careful."

As he walked away, Madeline looked back down at her computer. "How dare he tell me what to do? It's not his brother that was accused of a murder he didn't commit. I'm not interfering with the police; I'm working alongside them. I know they're busy, so I'm just trying to make sure they don't miss anything," she whispered to herself as she pulled open her emails.

Lunch came and went, and when she went back to her office, Detective Stephenson had called to set up an interview time with her that afternoon. They made plans to meet up at the field level seats to discuss the day of the murder even further. She was bursting to tell him the information she had found out but waited until he got settled into his seat and pulled his notebook out. Before she could launch into what she had told Davis earlier, he held up a hand interrupting her.

"Madeline, Davis already filled me in on what you found out. While I appreciate your enthusiasm, I wish you wouldn't involve yourself in our investigation. This could be a dangerous situation and we don't want anyone to get hurt. We're professionals, let us do our job. Now, for the real reason I'm here. Run me through that morning again from the time you arrived at the ballpark until the time you found the body of Mr. Dailey." He flipped to a blank page in his notebook and looked at her expectantly.

Fine. "I got up around seven in the morning, like usual. Putted around the house for a bit. Fed my cats, showered, changed, and drove into work around eightish. After settling into my office, I decided to take a walk around the field to clear my head. It's something I've done a lot since my Grandpa bought the team.

It was probably around eight-thirtyish." She paused, letting his writing catch up to her. He gestured her to continue.

"I saw Dave, the groundskeeper, working on the infield with some of his guys. We exchanged waves and he went back to his work. As I continued my walk on the third base side of the field, I noticed something shining from the visitors' dugout." She thought back to that moment and shuddered. "I wanted to check it out to make sure everything was okay over there."

The detective interrupted her. "Do you usually check in the dugouts on your morning walks?"

"No, not usually. But that day I saw something out of the ordinary. The dugouts are usually pretty dark places in the morning, nothing should be sparkling or shining." She rolled her eyes and then caught herself with a stricken expression. Probably not the best idea, because the detective gave her an admonishing look. Right, police. Probably not a good idea to irritate them. "So, when I saw something shining I went into the dugout. That's when I saw the body and the blood on the floor. I screamed, which was embarrassing, and called Dave over to phone 911. I made sure not to touch anything and ran upstairs to tell Davis what was going on."

With that, the detective looked up from his notebook and peered at her. "Why did you go to Davis immediately instead of waiting for the police to arrive?"

"Well, since he's head of security I figured he should know right away. He knows what to do in these weird types of situations. It turns out, Dave had called him over the walkies anyway and he already knew about the situation. After that, he walked me back down to the field and introduced me to you guys. You know the rest." She leaned back in her seat and looked out towards centerfield. The sun was shining, and some members of the team were still out running drills. She couldn't believe that all this was happening. It seemed surreal; this didn't usually happen to normal people.

Detective Stephenson leaned closer to her. "And you're sure you had never seen this man before?"

"No, I saw him, but I didn't know him. He was at the concessions party we had a few nights before his murder. He was talking to my brother about something, I don't know what about. I asked both my brother and Davis who the guy was, but they told me not to worry about it. So, I didn't." She sighed, looking at her watch. The shiny silver band twinkled in the sunlight and she thought back to what she saw in the dugout that day. "Are we almost done here? I have a lot to do before the park opens tomorrow to the public."

Detective Stephenson stood up, and Madeline followed his lead. "Okay, I think I have everything I need for now. But try to stay local so if I have any other questions I can reach you. Remember what I said; don't try to run around investigating this on your own. Leave it to the professionals." With that final salvo, he walked back towards the entrance to the offices. She assumed he had more people to talk to inside. Madeline decided to stay outside for a few more minutes to corral her racing thoughts.

It seemed to her that the police still didn't have a viable suspect in mind. She thought the guy was such a bad dude, one would think that there'd be no shortage of suspects who would want him dead. A former criminal con artist probably didn't make a lot of friends. And if he did have friends, they probably weren't the goody-two-shoes non-criminal type of people. She was sure there were more sketchy people in his life.

She walked down the aisle to the field level where the players were just heading into the dugout and locker room. It was about two in the afternoon, and she knew that Billy was taking them down to study some tape of the team that was coming in for the game the next day. The Foxboro Fanatics were another local team that boasted a pretty sizable following in the area. They had been the Armadillos Opening Day opponent for the last five years. The owner of that team was a good friend to her family and they mutually attended each other's events throughout the season. The Fanatics were another unaffiliated team, but they benefitted from being near where the New England Patriots played.

Since the field was empty, she saw Dave and his crew head out with rakes and other tools to get the final preps done on the field for the first game. She wanted to talk to Dave a bit more about that morning, even though the detective and Davis both told her to keep her nose out of this business. She couldn't help it. It was her family and her team. She wanted to help protect them.

She waved at Dave and beckoned him over to the first base side to talk. He handed his rake over to one of the young high school students who helped out during school breaks and summers. He jogged over and said a quick hello.

"Sorry to interrupt your work, Dave, but the field is looking great. I can't wait for tomorrow." Flattery always loosened people up in detective novels and TV shows. "Remember the morning of the murder? Do you recall seeing anything out of the ordinary?"

Dave looked at her with questions in his eyes. "The police already talked to me about that day. Twice actually. Why do you want to know?" He looked around the field and caught the eye of one of his employees who seemed to be slacking off, staring into space. The employee quickly stood up and got back to raking the pitcher's mound with a fervor not usually associated with high school students. Dave had that effect on the kids. Some of them didn't have proper parental figures at home, and Dave provided them with a safe space to work and enjoy the outdoors. Plus, it brought more kids to the game of baseball which the family loved. She saw how he interacted with the kids and they really respected him.

"It was just a weird morning, you know. I still can't believe I found a dead guy. Did you know him at all?" Madeline tried to sound as innocent as she could. Dave got a shifty look in his eyes and scratched his forehead distractedly. She could tell he was hiding something. Body language always gave people away. "Come on, Dave, you're a good guy. You don't have to worry about anything. You kind of give the impression that you might have known him."

He sighed and looked down. "Yeah, I sort of knew of him. I didn't know him personally. I heard some rumors that he might be in the habit of selling steroids to baseball players. I don't think it was any of our guys, but I heard from another team that he was caught hanging around their fields looking for players to talk to. I told Billy about it, just to make sure our guys didn't get caught up in the mess. He said he'd keep an eye on things. The guy was just a bad dude, Maddie." With that last statement, he turned and walked back to the pitcher's mound to relieve the kid with the rake.

Madeline's thoughts came fast and furious now, and she leaned against the home team dugout rail. Now that was interesting. Yes, another piece of the puzzle. He was a bookie, a scouting agent, and a steroid pusher? How many criminal careers could this guy have? And why was he at the field so early in the morning? It didn't sound like he had any connection to the team at the moment; could someone have been meeting him here to make the team look bad?

She stood straight up. That was an interesting thought. The Abington team was one of the more successful teams in the Northeast Regional Division. Granted, there were only three other teams, but the team consistently brought in the most talent and had the highest attendance. It didn't hurt that the team was close to the Cape Cod Baseball League and scouted players from those teams every summer. In all the leagues, there were players who would never, for whatever reason, make a big league club. They still loved the game, they loved to play, and this team gave them a chance to continue to live their dreams for a little while longer. She could definitely see a guy like Dailey preying on someone's dreams to get ahead. Especially if he was as bad a guy as everyone was making him out to be.

Chapter Six

Opening Day was a big deal. First of all, it was a day game held on a Saturday. That meant families could come without having to miss any work time. In early April, the weather could always be iffy. There could even be a snowstorm in April and sometimes even into May. New England was an interesting place.

The team lucked out this time with a beautiful day. The sun was shining, the temperature was supposed to be about 60 degrees at first pitch, and the field was glistening in the early morning sun. Madeline made it a point to be at the field early on her first official Opening Day back with the team. Even when she wasn't working with the team, she would try to get there early if she could. Her love for the game is what helped her to remain close to the family, and she was excited to start this new season as a full-fledged member of the family business.

That day she arrived at the ballpark bright and early at seven in the morning. There were only a few cars in the parking lot, mostly game day staff managers. The players wouldn't start to arrive until about nine for the pre-game workouts. First pitch would be around one-thirty. She pulled her bag out of the car and began the short walk to the front office doors. The door was located on the side of one of the main gated entrances of the ballpark. She noticed that one of the gates had a person standing in front of it peering into the empty ballpark. Since it was a small local team, there was never really a rush to buy tickets, or people lining up hours before the games. She looked to see if anyone else was around and started to head towards where the guy was standing.

As she got closer, he turned around, noticed her, and took off to the main road leading out of the stadium. In his haste to get out of there, he dropped a piece of paper on the ground in front of the gates.

"Hey! Are you okay? Did you need help? You dropped something!" she yelled after him. Bending down, she picked up the paper to see what it was. It was a note that said, "Meet me at the Abington Stadium if you want more."

More what? The note wasn't signed, and the paper didn't have any other information on it.

That was weird. The guy looked sort of familiar, too. Like someone she had seen recently. Actually, the more she thought about it, the more the guy sort of looked like the owner of the Barnstable Barnstormers. Last time she saw him was at the concessions party getting super sloppy drunk. He wouldn't have any reason to be here at the ballpark, especially before a game that his team wasn't even playing in. She stuffed the note in her pocket and made a mental note to tell Davis about it when she saw him next.

Madeline shrugged and pulled the door open to the offices. The first person she saw was Eliza, who was another person who loved to be at the field early on game days. She had started a pot of coffee for the office and was busy typing on the computer when she walked in. Eliza's long red nails tapped out a staccato rhythm that was oddly comforting to Madeline. After all the craziness, it was soothing to have things normal for a bit. She knew Eliza wasn't working yet, she tended to frequent her favorite TV shows in office downtime. She was an avid commenter on various plot points and even wrote her own fan fiction sometimes.

Madeline gave her a quick wave and scurried into her office and shut the door. Before she got too involved in Eliza's daily drama, she wanted to make sure everything was in place for the afternoon game. They had a middle school choir coming in to sing the national anthem. A parent of one of the kids was going to surprise them after singing to throw out the first pitch with his son. The parent had been stationed overseas for the past eight months. That kind of reunion was always good for some viral videos, and it made Madeline cry every time. It was going to be great.

About two hours later, more people had come into the office and things were starting to pick up. Madeline's brother, Ben, poked his head into her door and asked to speak with her. She waved him in with a flick of her hand. He came and shut the door behind him, sinking down into the extra chair in her office. He rubbed a hand over his face and sighed.

"Maddie. Man, it's been a crazy week. I don't think I'm a suspect anymore in that guy's murder, but the police have been hounding me non-stop. The only good thing in this whole mess is that it seems like the press haven't really been too tough on this one. I'm hoping it doesn't affect the attendance for today. We need to keep the attendance up otherwise we might have to start cutting back on a few things at the ballpark."

"Ben, you need to tell me everything you know about Christopher Dailey. Why were you fighting with him that night at the party? She leaned forward. Ben looked reluctant to tell her anything, so she kept pushing him to answer. "You owe me and the family that much. Since you're innocent, the fight you had shouldn't matter. Plus, I already know he wasn't a good guy, so nothing would be too surprising about him."

He rolled his eyes at her. "That's the understatement of the year. He was a complete jerk. I had talked to him during the winter; he contacted me out of the blue about signing some kid to a pretty lucrative contract for a pitcher. I told him that's not what we do. We are a small, unaffiliated team; we don't do 'lucrative.' We do adequate. Apparently, the guy he wanted me to sign was some hot shot at this college before being kicked out of school for honor code violations. I don't know much more about it. I told him to bug off. I hadn't heard from him again until the night of the party when he showed up trying to get me to reconsider the team position." Ben got up and headed towards the door. "I mean, he wasn't a good guy, but he didn't deserve to die the way he did. Hopefully, the police will figure out what's going on soon. And by the way, I know for a fact that Davis told you to stay out of it. So, you should probably take his advice.

He was halfway out the door when he turned around one more time. "Oh, and we're all set for the first pitch if you want to get out there and make sure the field is all set. The kids from the middle school should be getting here any time now."

Madeline looked at the clock and realized how close to the start time it actually was. She left the office quickly, checked in with her mom at the end of the hall to see if there were any fires to put out, and continued down towards the field. She leaned out over the first base wall and looked out towards centerfield. The field looked great, and the teams already had some guys out taking batting practice. Everything looked good. She spoke to the sound guy over the walkie talkie to make sure they were all set and then paged security to have them call her when the kids got there.

She headed back inside and went straight to Davis' office. He wasn't in there, so she took a Post-it note from his desk and told him to meet her on the concourse as soon as possible. She wanted to make sure the investigation was still progressing and also to give him the note the Barnstormer owner dropped this morning at the gate.

Madeline went back down to the concourse and began a walk around the perimeter. Most of the concession stands were in their set-up process. They didn't have a lot, but they had the three new stands plus the original hot dog, burger, and fries stand. Everything was setting up just fine. While she walked through the concourse, she couldn't help but think more about the Christopher Dailey case.

So, maybe he was a known bookie who might have been pushing steroids around local baseball teams and also represented some sort of baseball player. He was mad at her brother for not signing his guy, but he must have also had enemies from his side steroid business. She didn't know much about those drugs, but 'roid rage had sure been a thing for as long as she could remember. Maybe one of his customers killed him in a fit of anger. Maybe the guy who couldn't get a contract got mad and did it as revenge for not getting a contract.

As she was thinking, she wasn't looking where she was going and slammed straight into a brick wall of a man. She looked up and it was Davis. He grabbed her arms to keep her from falling backwards. She let out an "oh" and tried to get her bearings.

"Maddie, I know you were looking for me. Is everything okay?" He was still holding on her arms and looking into her eyes. Dang, he was cute. Those deep brown eyes, that dark chocolate-colored hair, she could definitely look at him forever. She shook herself out of her reverie and steadied herself.

"Yeah, I'm fine. Sorry about that." He pulled her over to the side of concourse to get out of the way of people hurrying back and forth. Once on the side, he let go of her arms and looked at Madeline questioningly. "I'm glad you found me. I have some more information for you regarding Christopher Dailey. Or at least I think it has something to do with it. Either way, it's weird."

"It's not like I'm going out of my way to get this information! I just ask questions and things tend to fall into my lap. I'm not skulking about or anything. Questions are all I'm asking." She rolled her eyes. "Anyway, did you know Chris was into selling steroids? Dave said he heard some guys talking about it, not from our team, but from others. That can't be a safe career. Oh! And this morning before I came into the office, William Chase of the Barnstormers was standing at the gate looking for something or someone. Before I could find out what he wanted, he took off running but not before dropping a piece of paper." She scrambled into her back pocket and pulled out a crumpled piece of notebook paper.

Davis looked at the paper closely for a few minutes and she could tell he was thinking about how it impacted everything going on. He folded the paper back up and put it in his shirt pocket. "I'll take this to the police and let them know about the strange behavior. And of course, they know about the steroid angle. Apparently, William had been on their radar for quite a while, mainly as a shady character, but had no proof of any illegal activity. Again, I have to say Maddie; you really should back away from this. From the steroid angle alone you could be in danger if someone thinks you know something. I just don't want to see you get hurt."

He looked to the side for a minute as if to see if anyone was listening to their conversation. Madeline looked around too to see if there was anything interesting happening, but not seeing anything worth noticing, she turned back to Davis.

He sighed, looked down, and then looked back up at her. "Look, after the game today, do you want to get a drink at Centerfields? It's a ritual the security team does every year after the first game. I'd like for you to come. I know the gala is tonight, but you'll be back before it even starts." Davis looked into her eyes and she felt a little frisson of electricity skate up her spine.

While not the most experienced with men since she hit her thirties, she had dated through college and went on a few dates while in the corporate world. She never really had a serious relationship though, but she thought Davis was flirting. Then again, maybe he was just being nice. Either way, she knew after the week she had, drinks were definitely needed. "Sure, I'd love to join you guys. As long as they don't mind the boss' daughter tagging along." She smiled at him. He smiled back and his shoulders seemed to relax a bit.

He nodded. "Great, we meet about an hour after the gates close. See you there. Good luck today and remember what I said about being careful." He looked at her once more before turning on his heels and walking back towards the front offices.

Madeline glanced as her watch and realized how close it was to gates being opened. At the same time, her walkie-talkie cackled and she heard Eliza's voice. "Madeline, Madeline. Come in. The singers have arrived. Madeline. I repeat. The singers have arrived. Over and out."

She shook her head laughing out loud. Eliza never really got the hang of the walkie-talkies. She always made it seem like they were cops or long-haul truckers. Madeline scurried down the concourse to meet the middle schoolers at the side gate. Let the games begin.

Chapter Seven

"...and the home of the brave." The little voices ended to a large round of applause. Madeline lined them up in the batter's box at home plate for parents to get pictures and for the kids to wave to the crowd. Right before they left the field, she pointed at the kid whose dad was going to surprise him. She handed him a ball and told him he was going to throw the first pitch. A man came out of the dugout with a catcher's mask on and squatted down behind home plate. The young man lobbed it into the air where the catcher caught it right in front of home plate. As he made his way to the kid to give him the ball, he whipped off his mask revealing himself to be the kid's father.

They ran into each other's arms, and Madeline wiped the tears from eyes. After the pictures were taken and the kids were taken off the diamond, she looked over at Billy and gave him the high sign. He knew that once the field was cleared, he could send out his pitcher to get a few warm-up throws off the mound before the game officially started.

The pitcher was a young guy fresh out of college who didn't quite have the stuff to pitch in the Cape League over the summer. The team still thought of him as good enough for the Armadillos. He was scouted by one of the team's most reliable guys, and they had high hopes for him. He worked for the minimum salary, but loved pitching, so making him Opening Day starter was a no-brainer. This was his first season with the team, and there were hopes that he would blossom into one of the most popular players on the Armadillos.

It was funny how she had only been working with the team for a few weeks, but it felt like she had been there forever. She never knew how much she liked working with her family and as part of the team until she had left for a bit. She took her time walking the concourse to the right field bleacher seats which is where she wanted to watch the game from. Every now and then they had a family watch party in the boxes by the press room, but most of the time they all went their separate ways as soon as the game started. Madeline liked to watch from the outfield because it gave a wider perspective to the game as a whole. A person could see every base, every decision by a runner, and there was even the possibility of grabbing a home run ball. Her brother preferred to sit behind home plate with the scouts. Her mother stayed in the office and listened to the game on the radio and put out any fires that arose during the game. Her father, on the other hand, sat in the press box. He liked the energy of the room and it also had one of the best views of the whole field.

The Boucher's were a family of baseball freaks. She knew her dad was grooming her brother to eventually take over as the head of baseball operations, but Madeline knew she wanted to stay a part of the business too. She had made a decision that before the season ended, she wanted to talk to her parents about possibly taking on a larger role in the organization. So far, the social media stuff had been going well even though it had only been a few weeks. She remembered everything her Grandpa had ever taught her about the game, and she couldn't imagine leaving it behind again. She couldn't even remember why she was so apprehensive about returning in the first place.

Settling against the railing in the standing room only section of right field, she took in the scene around her. The stadium fit 3,000 people, and on most games days they topped out around 2,000. Since today was Opening Day, it looked like a full crowd and she estimated that the stadium was at least mostly full. The team had lucked out in the weather and it being on a Saturday afternoon. There were lots of families interspersed throughout the park, along with the old timers who had been attending games forever. This would hopefully be a great season as long as they could keep the attendance up. She was going to make extra sure the social media side staying clued in and made trips to the ballpark fun.

Madeline caught the eye of an older man, probably in his seventies a few rows from the top. He waved at her enthusiastically. He was one of the team's season ticket holders. He had been coming to the park since the early seventies, even before her family owned the team. He pointed excitedly to the young boy sitting next to him in the row. She assumed it was his grandson and she waved at both of them. She was so happy to see the generations together at the park. She remembered watching games like that with her grandpa.

She snapped out of her observations with the crack of the bat. She saw a ball sailing out towards the right field bleachers where she was standing. The right fielder scrambled backwards but watched the ball clear the fence over his head. At this point in the game, the Armadillos had a quick top of the first, the pitcher retiring the Foxboro team in order. The home run in the bottom of the first inning came courtesy of the Armadillos veteran player, David Murphy. He had been playing with the team for the previous five years and was the favorite player of many fans.

The crowd was losing their minds, screaming and clapping ecstatically. Three rows in front of where Madeline was standing was a young family. The youngest boy held up the ball in his glove. A nice souvenir from the ballpark. Madeline walked down the aisle to where he and his family were sitting.

She handed them her card, "Hey, young man. Great catch! I work with the team. Would you like to come down to the field after the game and run the bases?" The little boy looked to be about six years old and nodded at her. She looked up at his parents. "If it's okay with you, of course. I'll just take the name of your party and after the last out, you can meet me down by the side of the home team dugout."

After collecting their names and promising to meet them afterwards, she went back to the railing for the next few innings. The Armadillos were up by a score of 5–1 in the sixth inning when she decided to walk around the concourse again to see how operations were going. Most of the families she encountered through the ballpark had big smiles on their faces and seemed to be enjoying themselves. She had high hopes for the rest of the season.

As she continued walking, she felt eyes on her back. She turned around quickly but didn't notice anyone paying her any particular attention. There was a family hanging out by the water fountain, two men in line at the beer stand, and a woman bending down to talk to her son at the entrance to the field-level seats. Even though no one seemed to be paying attention to her, she still felt the uncomfortable sensation of someone watching her. It was creepy. She tried to shrug it off and continued walking to the front of the ballpark. She arrived by the front gates and took a look back at the crowded concourse.

She felt a tap on her shoulder. Standing there was William Chase, owner of the Barnstormers. He certainly looked like the guy she saw this morning, but he did not give her any indication that he saw her earlier that day. Last time they were this close to each other, William was three sheets to the wind at the party. Not known for his restraint, she and William never really spoke to each other. They didn't exactly travel in the same circles.

William had been owner of the Barnstormers for the previous five years. He came from family money, but also ended up creating some sort of app that tracked baseball players through their careers. She wasn't 100% sure what the app actually did, but she did know that it made him a ton of money. So, what else would a guy do when he gets lot of money? Buy a sports team. He wasn't known for his good looks, of that she was sure. He was in his early forties with salt and pepper hair. He wasn't tall, but he wasn't short either. Just kind of average. Not very athletic in the least, a bit pudgy around his middle from years of sitting behind computers and desks. And he sweat. Profusely. Probably from the drinking.

"Madeline Boucher? Right?" He looked at her. She didn't know how he knew to find her at this exact moment.

"Yeah, I'm Madeline. Can I help you with something?" She tried to keep suspicion out of her voice. She kept a hand on the walkie-talkie clipped to her front pocket just in case things took a turn south. She tried not to breathe too deeply since the smell of alcohol seemed to permeate his pores. His eyes looked a little bit too red for an early afternoon baseball game. Especially since his team had their own home opener that night on the Cape. Why would he be there at 2:30 p.m., when he should be at his own ballpark preparing?

He looked around the crowded area and leaned closer. "You know, I was very concerned when I heard about the misfortune you guys experienced last week."

Madeline instinctively took a step back to get out of the range of his breath. What a weird way to describe a murder, a misfortune.

"I just wanted to see if you needed anything from me going forward. We baseball owners have to stick together," he continued.

Madeline was concerned that he was dangerously close to invading her personal space. Why would he come to her with this? "I think you should talk to my Dad. Maybe during regular business hours? He would know better what and if we need anything. The police are investigating and we're just trying to get on with the season."

She nodded at him and backed away to emphasize that her part in the conversation was over. Before she could get away, he grabbed her arm. She shook his hand off and looked at him incredulously. Before she could lay into him, she saw Davis approaching out of the corner of her eye. He caught her eye and lifted a brow in question. She shrugged and rolled her eyes in William's direction.

"Mr. Chase, Ms. Boucher. How is everything over here?" Davis slowly walked up and casually put himself in between William and herself. "Games almost over, you ready to start closing things out?" He looked at her, giving her an out to the conversation.

"Yes, great. I have some after game things planned for some fans, so I should get to it. Nice talking to you, Mr. Chase." She darn near ran away from the two men as fast as she could. Glancing over her shoulder, she saw the two men deep in conversation with William poking Davis in the chest. She wondered what that was all about and made a mental reminder to ask Davis about it at the bar that night.

After most home games, especially the ones played during the day, a majority of the players hung out in the dugout to meet with kids and families. She grabbed some swag bags of stuff for the home run kid which included a mini-bat, jersey, and tickets to an upcoming game. She hurried down to the entrance of the home team dugout seats and waited for the last out to be called.

"STRIKE THREE!" The umpire emphatically called out the Foxboro player looking on a change-up from the closer. The crowd went crazy and the team began high-fiving each other in the dugout and on the field. Much like their Boston neighbors, the Red Sox, the team played "Dirty Water" by the Standells after every game. It made a person feel like they were watching a big league team play for a lot less money.

As people streamed towards the exits, Madeline waded her way through the crowd down to field level. She gave a quick wave to the team and waited for the family to arrive. About ten minutes after the last out was called, the family with the home run kid approached. She handed the little boy and his siblings bags of goodies and congratulated him again on a great catch. She led the family through a side gate next to the dugout onto the field. Some of the players were still hanging around, including the player who hit the home run.

"Hey! David!" She called, waving him over. The little boy got an excited look on his face and grabbed the ball he caught from his father. "This little fan caught your first inning home run ball. How would you like to take him on a trip around the bases?"

David smiled at the kid and his family. "Of course! And when we get back, I'll make sure to sign that ball for you." He took the kid by the hand and led him towards home plate. The parents quickly grabbed their cellphones and started taping the whole interaction. Madeline had called up to the videographers of the game to make sure they captured this for the website later.

Davis chased the boy around the bases and even gave him a signed bat on the way off the field. The kid couldn't stop smiling from ear to ear. Even his parents looked a little awed by the whole experience. She led the family towards the front gate, with them thanking her the entire way out for the experience. She let them know that it wasn't a problem, and that the team couldn't wait to see them at a future game. She gave the little boy a handshake and waved as he skipped his way through the parking lot.

Smiling, Madeline turned to head back to her office. She again got the feeling that someone was watching her. She didn't see anyone earlier, but maybe now with the thinner crowd she could spot the person giving her the creepy feeling. She pulled her cellphone out of her pocket and pretended to check emails while turning slowly in a circle. She tried surreptitiously glancing off the screen to see if she could notice anyone paying special attention to her.

There! A dude with his hat pulled down over his eyes was definitely glancing up every few seconds at her. Come to think of it, he looked sort of familiar too. It was definitely the guy that Tom was arguing with behind right field the other day. She pretended to keep checking her cell phone as she began walking nonchalantly towards him. As soon as she got within ten feet however, he took off in the other direction at a steady brisk walk. Not a run, but still fast enough that she couldn't call out to him before he made it to the exit gate.

She shivered. Super creepy. Some rando watching her while she worked. Well, just one more thing she would have to tell Davis about at happy hour. She walked back to her office to make sure everything was on track for the next few days. After happy hour was the season ticket party, and she was glad that she brought her dress to change into later, that way she didn't have to rush home. Opening Day was always the hardest day of the season, but now that it was over, she had confidence the rest of the season would run smoothly. She had a few emails from people wondering if there was any information on the murder, but after quick searches, she found they were all local reporters. She sent back a standard reply that the police were investigating and all other questions should be directed to them.

Madeline looked up and glanced at her clock, saw it was approaching four and knew it was about time to head over to the restaurant. She ran a quick comb through her hair and pulled it back in a headband, popped some mascara on her eyelashes, and grabbed her purse. Stopping to say goodbye to her parents, she swiftly exited the offices and headed towards Centerfields.

Chapter Eight

Madeline arrived at Centerfields within two minutes of leaving her office. One benefit of the restaurant being attached to the stadium was the proximity to the office so Happy Hour could get started quickly. Entering the lobby of the bar, she looked around to see if the security team had made it over yet. In the back of the bar where there were pool tables and dart boards, she saw Davis waving her over. She picked her way through the early evening crowd, many of whom were at the game earlier, to the group of people in the back.

Next to Davis were two guys from his security team. Playing darts was the only female member of his team, Esther. While her name implied an elderly woman, Esther was actually in her late twenties and one of her oldest friends. After leaving school she joined the local police force. After several years there, she decided to quit and start a family with her high school sweetheart husband. Security detail with the Abington Armadillos provided her with the chance to use her skills but the schedule was much less demanding so she could spend time with her family.

Esther looked over as Madeline joined the group and came running over with her arms outstretched. "Maddie! It's so good to see you! I've been on vacation so I was sad to miss your first couple of days. I heard it was exciting!"

Madeline smiled at her friend and rolled her eyes. "Yeah, real exciting. Finding a dead body and then my brother becoming a suspect. All leading up to the most important day of the season, Opening Day. So yeah, exciting would definitely be a good way to describe it." She gestured to the bartender and ordered a glass of Pinot Grigio, her wine of choice. She made a pact with herself only to have one drink with the security team; she had a busy night still ahead of her with the season ticket gala and wanted to keep her eye on the ball. Metaphorically speaking, of course.

The guys racked up a quick game of pool, so they split into two teams. Esther and Madeline on one side, Davis and his friend/co-worker Brandon on the other. After a few quick games of pool, the guys accepted their losses and they all retreated to the high top tables piled with appetizers. The group talked about the success of the day when Esther checked her phone and jumped up.

"Guys, I hate to be the first to leave, but Danny's picking me up with the kids now. See you all in the morning!" She grabbed her bag and exited out the front of the restaurant.

Once Esther had left, the party started to wind down until Davis and Madeline were the only two people left. They made their way to the front door where he stopped her with a hand on her arm. Standing outside the door in the cool spring air, it almost felt like they had been on a date and he was about to kiss her goodnight. Just her overactive imagination.

"Maddie, I wanted to let you know that it looks like your brother will no longer be a true suspect in Chris Dailey's murder. From what he told me, he has a pretty decent alibi. He was out for drinks the night before and went home to pass out. He mentioned something about a meeting in the morning not in Abington, so I think he was away from the ballpark when the murder occurred. He doesn't really have any reason to lie to me, so I'm going to take him at his word. We can now try to get on with our lives and let the police do the dirty work of finding the actual culprit."

Madeline smiled at Davis. "That's good news. But, well, I did want to ask you about what you and William Chase were arguing about at the game. I'm glad you rescued me when you did; he seemed pretty drunk and out of control. But then he looked pretty agitated with you, too."

Davis sighed and shook his head. "You just can't help yourself, can you? He was mad because I interrupted you guys. He said he had something really important to tell you. Do you have any idea what he meant? I told him to make an appointment through Eliza during business hours."

She tapped her chin and tried to think about what he would've wanted to tell her. "No, I can't think of any business I have with that guy. Maybe he saw me pick up that note he dropped this morning and wanted it back. It just seemed weird that he was at our game this afternoon when he has a game himself tonight."

"Look, I have to get going. You have my cell, right?" Madeline nodded at him. "Call me if you need something or if anything weird happens again to you. There are things in this mess I'm just not sure about and I would rather not spend my time worrying about you." Davis looked at her for a charged minute, patted her on the arm and turned towards the parking lot. "See you at the gala tonight. I'm running home first and I'll be back."

She watched him walk away. She decided that after things calmed down and the season was in full swing, she was going to ask him on a proper date. Go big or go home. She resolved to tell Eliza all about this afternoon's excitement at the first chance she got.

Madeline gathered her purse over her arm and decided she had time to go back to the office before the gala started. She could change in her office. Before she could push the door open, a woman wrenched the door from her hand and came barreling into her. The woman was a bit older than Madeline with stringy blonde hair, heavy black eye make-up, fake tan, long nails, and the works. She ran into the lobby of the restaurant, banged into Madeline, and went sprawling. As she fell backwards, her purse went flying in the air and landed on some seats next to the hostess stand. Madeline reached down to help her up and noticed she was crying.

"Ma'am, I'm sorry, are you okay? Let me help you with your stuff." Madeline grabbed the woman's purse and started shoving things that had fallen out into it. The woman sat on the floor of the restaurant crying. Looking down at all her things strewn about the floor, Madeline wondered who she was. She had lipstick, mascara, a prescription bottle, loose tissues, a pack of cigarettes, and a hastily bundled together pack of notes. She shoved everything in the bag and went to grab the woman's arm.

The woman jerked her arm away from her and stood up unsteadily. "I'm fine. It's just a bad week that's all." She wiped her hand across her face. "My boyfriend was murdered here at the stadium and no one wants to help me get information. They keep telling me to go to the police. But the police are no help at all! I just want to know what happened!" Her voice got steadily louder until she was yelling and creating a scene in the lobby of the restaurant. People leaned out of their booths to see what the ruckus was about.

Madeline looked over at the hostess and pointed at a corner booth out of the way of the main entrance. She nodded and Madeline led the woman over to the empty seats. She settled her down into the booth and grabbed the closest waiter. "Can I get a coffee for this lady? I'll pay for it, just bring it quickly."

He scurried off in the direction of the kitchen. She looked back at the lady in the booth who was alternating sobbing loudly and sniffling into her napkins. Madeline knew she should probably leave it alone, but her innate curiosity pulled her in the direction of the sobbing woman. She might know more about why Chris was killed. If the police didn't want to help her, the least Madeline could do was listen. And if she found anything out, she could pass it on to Davis and the police immediately.

She sat down across from the woman and put on her best sympathetic face. "I'm Maddie, are you sure you're okay by yourself?" She made eye contact with the weeping woman and tried to convey understanding.

The woman sniffled into her napkin. "Thanks for helping me back there. It's just frustrating to not have answers, you know?"

Madeline nodded.

"It sucks to have someone you know and cared about murdered. It wasn't like he was that bad of a guy. He was cleaning up his act for sure. By the way, my name is Ashley, did you know Chris?" She looked at Madeline with mascara tracks on her face.

Uh-oh. Madeline didn't want to tell her that she was the one who found Chris' body. That might just push her over the edge. She wondered if there was a plausible story she could tell Ashley to help her open up more.

"Um, well, I didn't know him all that well. He was friends with my brother, Ben." Not a complete lie. She rationalized that they knew each other so they might have been friends in another life. Just at this moment, they weren't anything before Chris was killed. Other than apparently fighting over baseball stuff.

"Ben? I think I know that name." Ashley sniffled and blew her nose again. "Either way, I know Chris had his issues, but he was always good to me. He couldn't help it if people were always expecting the worst of him!" She grabbed another pile of napkins but before she could burst into another round of tears, her coffee was unceremoniously plopped down in front of her. The waiter hightailed it away from the crying lady without checking to see if there was anything else they needed.

"Why don't you tell me a little bit more about Chris? It might help you feel better." Madeline crossed her fingers under the table. She hoped that Ashley would take the cue and spill her guts about her boyfriend. She didn't seem suspicious of Madeline asking all these questions, so Madeline decided to press her advantage as much as possible.

Ashley leaned back into the booth with a heavy sigh. "Chris and I met a few years ago. He had just gotten out of prison for some gambling thing, I think. He was so sweet. We met at the packie down by my house. I live in South Boston." She got a dreamy look in her eye, but she had stopped crying. "He picked me up right then and there. We fell in love almost immediately. He wasn't a bad guy, he really wasn't."

She grabbed Madeline's hand, pleading. "He just fell into the wrong crowd. I know he was trying to get straight and not get involved in the whole gambling thing again. He promised he had changed. And now I can't even get the police to tell me anything because I'm not 'family.'" She held up air quotes as she said the last word with a disgusted look on her face.

Even though Madeline did not have the best feelings towards Chris, she felt bad for the poor woman. Obviously, she thought he was a good guy and was now having a hard time dealing with his death. Madeline couldn't imagine how that felt. Losing someone to an act of violence must be hard. Then being shut out of information? That must feel ten times worse. Plus, Madeline had a feeling that Ashley had a hard life and that little bit of happiness with Chris was special for her.

Madeline patted the woman's hand. "I'll see what I can find out for you. I'm friends with someone who knows things about the case. Can you think of anything, of anyone, who might want to hurt Chris? I can pass that information along if you don't feel comfortable talking to the police."

Ashley shredded the napkins in her hand. "The police already spoke to me once. I gave them as much information as I could. He didn't really introduce me to any of his friends. I mean, I met some at a game we went to in Barnstable, but he said they were just some guys he grew up with. WAIT!" She looked up at Madeline with surprise in her eyes. "Something weird did happen the other day."

Madeline sat up straighter, thinking it might be important. She felt like maybe she was about to bust this thing wide open.

Ashley continued. "We were down on the Cape walking along the beach when Chris got a phone call. He walked away saying it was business. I heard him yelling into the phone something about a shipment not being received on time. I didn't think anything about it because he was always working on something. But he sounded really angry. When I asked him about it later, he said it was nothing to worry about. Just some guy not doing his job correctly. So, I let it go. Looking back, maybe it was something serious." She started crying again.

Madeline looked around the crowded restaurant to see if anyone was making a move to help her with the weeping woman. Everyone in the restaurant avoided her gaze.

Madeline cleared her throat. "I think you should call the police and tell them that story. It could be important. Maybe they'll even give you more information." Madeline looked at the woman who was putting a mound of napkins against her face. "Ashley, is there anyone I can call to help you get home? You seem upset and I don't want you driving around on your own."

Ashley blew her nose again and pulled out her cell phone, looking down at the texts that had just come through. "It's okay. My friend AJ is on her way here and should be meeting me soon." She grabbed Madeline's hand. "Thank you so much for listening. It has just been a lot. I need some sort of closure, otherwise it's like Chris won't get any justice. I couldn't handle that."

Madeline patted the woman's hand and pulled a business card out of her pocket. Luckily it wasn't her team cards. She still had cards printed from her last job. For some reason she didn't want Ashley to think she was fishing for information to use against her for the protection of the team. "Ashley, if you need anything, don't hesitate to call me."

She grabbed the card out of Madeline's hand and looked up at her gratefully. Looking behind Madeline, she waved at someone approaching the table.

"Be safe, Ashley." Madeline headed towards the front. All told, that little detour cost her another hour. It was now only about half an hour before the gala was set to start. Standing in the front of restaurant, she rummaged in her purse for her keys. Something on the floor caught her eye. It was a piece of paper, crumpled in a ball. She laughed a little. Second piece of paper today that she found. Picking it up, she found it had the same handwriting as other things Ashley had in her purse. Opening the paper fully, she found that it was a list of names. Some were crossed out, others had stars next to them. One thing they had in common? They were all on Madeline's list of suspects in Chris Dailey's murder.

Granted, she wasn't the police, so she probably shouldn't have a suspect list. She just couldn't let it go. Maybe it was the years of mystery reading, but she really felt she could help in the investigation. People liked her; they'd talk to her more readily than the police. She couldn't be in any danger yet. She just started, so she shook off a little fissure of unease and stuffed the list into her purse and headed back to the office.

Chapter Nine

Madeline hurried back to her office to change into her gala dress. No time to investigate that list she found, so she stuffed it into the top drawer of her desk and grabbed the dress hanging on the back of the door. The gala itself tended to be pretty casual, no big ball gowns, no tuxedos, no super fancy jewelry. Unless the ticket holders wanted to go that fancy of course. Madeline chose a black tea length cocktail dress and a team scarf wrapped around her neck. She was thankful she had remembered to bring her outfit to the ballpark that day. She would've been late otherwise.

After a quick change behind her desk, she took out a compact mirror and made sure her face and hair were on point. Deciding that she looked good enough for the gala, she grabbed a black clutch and threw a few things in to tide her over for the night. The gala was only supposed to go until eleven, so she hoped to be back home by midnight. She also hoped that the event wouldn't be marred by all the hoopla surrounding the murder, but she knew how gossip tended to spread in a small town.

She made her way back out into the hallway and caught up with her parents as they proceeded to the event space. Like the concessions party, they were holding the event on the concourse. Food and drink were set up at several concession stands and white shirt clad waiters were walking around with appetizers for people to enjoy. Music was provided by the team DJ, a kid who attended college nearby, and the place looked like it was filling up when they arrived.

Madeline followed behind her parents as they entered the party area. Ben was already there, schmoozing with the guests with a drink in his hand. When the crowd saw her parents, they gave a hearty round of applause. Her dad walked to the small podium set up near the booths and waved a hand to acknowledge the applause.

"I want to thank you all for coming tonight and supporting your Abington Armadillos as we begin our season. We had a great game today and hope to continue with the great season we have planned. You are the supporters that provide us with joy and love every year, and so we thank you. Enjoy the party and enjoy the season." He stepped from behind the microphone and walked off towards his wife to the sound of applause.

Gradually everyone went back to their own conversations. Madeline tried to eavesdrop as much as she could to what people were saying. She figured it wouldn't hurt to see what the gossip about the murder was.

About fifty people were at the party, a majority of them older folks who have followed the team for a while. There weren't many opportunities to own season tickets for sporting events in the area, and the Red Sox were a hefty price tag for some people. Plus, access wasn't that great either. This way, they got the best seats at low prices, and got to see some stars of the future play in the area. The team also provided a chance for aging MLB veterans to continue their careers a little longer after they washed out of the majors. It was a fascinating group of players, and Madeline found a lot of their stories interesting.

Madeline couldn't remember why she was so hesitant to come back to the team before. The people at the ballpark were nice, the fans that came out to the games were exceptional, and all her co-workers made her feel welcome right away. The only thing marring her return was the murder of Chris Dailey. Her family was acting pretty normal even though their son was a possible suspect in a murder. There was no other family drama outside of the murder, and she had been enjoying herself in the lead up to the opening of the season. Maybe working for the family business thing could work permanently. She knew her grandpa would've loved to have the team stay a family affair for as long as possible.

Madeline grabbed a glass of wine and snagged a slider off of one of the passing waiter's trays. She was glad she didn't drink too much at happy hour earlier. White wine was her weakness and, if left unchecked, she would have quite a hangover in the morning. She wanted to stay sharp just in case she heard any gossip that could help her investigation.

As she circled the small party area, she picked up on a few conversations. Most of them concerned family updates or local events. Madeline thought that was a good sign, no one was talking about her family or the murder. She bobbed her head along to the music that the DJ was playing. The family had made sure he mixed it up between current hits and classics for some of the older patrons. No one seemed to mind the music. Several couples were already dancing on the makeshift dance floor on the concourse.

Madeline glanced over at her parents. She saw they were deep in conversation with someone who looked sort of familiar. She couldn't quite place where she had seen him before though. He looked to be about her age, tall, dark hair, and an ice gray summer suit. Catching her mother's eye, she waved Madeline over with a smile on her face.

Uh-oh. Madeline knew that look. It had to be a possible matchmaking trick. It was her mother's specialty. She hoped the guy didn't turn out to be a complete dud like the accountant she set her up with a few years ago. Not that all accountants were bad, just that numbers bored her and so had this particular guy.

Madeline weaved her way through the crowd and approached her mother. The guy turned around and reached out a hand to introduce himself. Now she remembered him. It was Tom, the scout from the other day. He was much cuter up close and not being screamed at by an old baseball dad.

"Madeline, this is Tom, one of our scouts. Tom, this is our daughter, Madeline, who put everything together for the game and this party." Her mother introduced the two of them with a smile on her face. "Oh, would you look over there." She pointed vaguely in the opposite direction. "I see a friend that I must simply talk to right now. You kids have fun." She patted Madeline on the arm and flitted off. Talk about transparent.

"So," Madeline said. "That wasn't too obvious, was it?"

Tom smiled back at her. "I get it. My mom's always trying to meddle in my life, too. My mom is constantly telling me about people in her office that would be perfect for me. I prefer to rely on my own skills to meet someone. That said, it's nice to officially meet you, Madeline."

They spent the rest of the party chatting in a corner. She found out that Tom was a really good guy. He spent his free time coaching little league baseball and tried to volunteer as much as he could at the local animal shelter as well. His parents lived in the area and he made sure to visit them for Sunday dinner every week. He was perfect. Almost too perfect.

Then, he dropped the bomb.

"So, you're the one who found the body the other day?"

Madeline started in surprise and looked at Tom with narrowed eyes. "Um, yeah. I didn't know that was common knowledge though."

He laughed, disarming her suspicion. "No, it's not. I was talking to your brother the other day and he mentioned it. I'm not some creepy guy who is obsessed with the situation. I was just wondering how weird that must have been to find a guy bludgeoned in the ballpark. I mean, he wasn't a good guy, but no one deserves to die like that."

Madeline relaxed a little. "Oh yeah, it was weird alright. I didn't know him at all, but it was the last thing I was expecting to see in this place." She shuddered as she thought back to that day.

"Do they have any idea who did it? I've heard rumors that he was involved in a lot of shady stuff in the baseball world. I think he was seen around the Barnstable team a couple of weeks ago talking to some people. Not a team-sanctioned conversation. In fact, I think security chased him off." Tom shrugged. "I also had a couple of people tell me he promised them tryouts with several teams without anything to back it up. Some kids went to the ballparks and were turned away. It was a huge scandal in our world."

Madeline took this information and filed it away for future investigation. She added to the mental list along with the list of people she still had in her office drawer. Before she could ask Tom any more questions, he looked at his watch.

"Oh, crap. I have to go. Early tomorrow with the little league. Hopefully we can get together for a coffee or something soon. I'll talk to you later." He handed her his business card and gave a jaunty wave before heading to the exit.

She took the card in her hands and twirled it between her fingers. She thought he just asked her out on a date. And she wasn't completely adverse to the idea. Davis didn't seem like he was all that interested in starting a relationship, and she couldn't wait around forever for him. Tom seemed like a good guy. Now she'd never hear the end of it from her mother. Especially if it turned into something serious.

Of course, thinking about Davis reminded Madeline of the note she found earlier. She thought he was going to be here tonight to tell him all about it, but apparently, he pawned the security for the event off to some of his underlings. She thought about maybe leaving a note for him to come talk to her in the morning on Monday. This stuff could probably wait until then.

The party seemed to be winding down, so she took the opportunity to sneak off to the front office. The office hallway was quiet with only a few low-level lights on for emergency purposes. Madeline shivered. It was a little bit creepy. She could imagine someone sneaking up behind her in the dark. She knew that there were people still around because of the party, but with the murder, every dark corner seemed potentially sinister. She wanted to hurry up and leave Davis the note and get the heck out of there. As she wrote the note in her office, she heard a noise from her brother's office on the other side of the hallway.

Taking her shoes off, she crept along as silently as she could, not wanting to get caught in case it was someone out to do harm. The team didn't keep any money or anything stored on site, the money was deposited after every game so they didn't have cash lying around for long periods of time.

The light was off in his office, so she figured it wasn't her brother doing some extra work. Before she could reach the doorway of his office, someone outside the window cleared their throat. She turned towards the sound and whoever was in Ben's office took off out the side door of the front office. She tried to follow after them, see if she could get a glimpse of who it was. She made it as far as the door before realizing she couldn't run across the parking lot shoeless.

She did think she caught a quick glimpse of the person, not that it mattered it was so dark out. She thought they were about her height, but they were wearing all black and a black hat. She couldn't even tell if it was man or woman who she saw. She sniffed the air around her. There was a smell that seemed familiar, like a cologne or perfume that she was sure she smelled before. Unfortunately, her sense of smell and memory weren't very good, because as hard as she thought, she couldn't figure out where she remembered it from.

Madeline sighed and put her shoes back on as she trudged back down the hallway. She turned the light on in her brother's office and found it torn apart. Papers were shuffled about, his guest chairs were tipped over, and she couldn't tell if anything had been taken. She went back to her office and grabbed her phone. Texting her brother down at the party, she let him know that she disturbed someone breaking into his office. Not two minutes later, he was by her side looking through his papers to see if the intruder took anything.

The safe in his office held important contract documents for players, and team finance information, but it didn't look disturbed at all. Instead, it just looked as if someone rooted through the papers on his desk and knocked some things over.

"I don't know, Maddie. I don't think there was anything important here. Stuff that would be worth breaking into an office for are in the safe. And that's still locked up tight." Ben ran a hand through his short dark hair in frustration.

They righted the chairs and took a seat across from each other in the office. Ben looked at her with concern in his eyes. "Are you okay, though?"

Madeline shuddered as she thought about the person running in the dark of the parking lot. She didn't even think twice about trying to catch up with them until she hit the blacktop. Probably not one of her best ideas. She had no clue if the person was dangerous or not, but she wanted some answers. They decided to seal off the office for the night and talk to the detectives and Davis in the morning. They seemed to be back where they started without any answers.

Chapter Ten

Due to the excitement of the last few days, sleep was not immediately forthcoming when Madeline got home that night. Her cats looked at her with disbelief as she kept tossing and turning in her bed. Finally, they gave up on her and found other cozy places to curl up for the night

Her Sunday was uneventful, and she took the time to get house things done. Three cats could cause havoc, and there was a lot of cat hair to vacuum and clean up. She caught up on all her shows, finished laundry, and was back in bed early before the start of the new workweek.

Rising at five in the morning, she grabbed an iced tea from the fridge. She wasn't a coffee drinker, but she definitely needed something to perk her up. She also needed the fortification to face Davis after the break-in the previous night. She probably should have called him as soon as it happened. But if she was honest, she wasn't in the mood to hear a lecture about how she should be more careful.

Madeline hopped into the shower, hoping it would help wake her up a bit. She decided to go casual for the day since there wasn't a game being played and no big appointments she had to worry about. Pulling on jeans and a team shirt, she shoved her hair back with a headband and headed out the door. First and foremost, she had to pick up her morning iced tea from the Dunkin' Donuts on the way to the ballpark. Just for fun she also picked up some munchkins for the office as well.

In her pocket she carried the piece of paper she found on the floor of the restaurant. It was hard to believe that it was only the day before. So much had happened since then. She wanted to talk it over with Davis before handing it off to the police. She wanted to help Ashley get closure if she could. But why was Ashley carrying around that piece of paper? It definitely looked like a list of suspects. Plus, she also needed to tell Davis about the break-in if he didn't already know.

Madeline got into her office after saying a quick hello to Eliza and spread the paper on the desk. She copied it over to another sheet of paper so she could have her own copy when she handed it over to the police. She picked up the phone and dialed Davis' interoffice extension.

"Davis, can you come here for a minute? I need to tell you about something that happened at the restaurant after you left yesterday. Also, something happened during the gala that you need to know about."

Davis promised to get there in a minute, and she hung up the phone. He didn't sound angry at her, so hopefully he didn't know about her near miss last night. She leaned back in her office chair to think. Was Ashley investigating her boyfriend's murder? Why didn't she go to the police if she had suspicions? Of course, she thought he was on the straight and narrow, but if that was the case, why did she have a list of people who all apparently hated Chris?

Davis walked into her office wearing a casual outfit of jeans and a nicely pressed button-down shirt. No T-shirts and cargo shorts for this guy. Madeline wondered if he had a girlfriend who helped take care of him. She hated to perpetuate stereotypes, but it was rare to see a man looking that good knowing how to work an iron.

She shook herself out of her fawning of Davis and realized she was staring at him. Clearing her throat, she gestured to the other chair and shuffled some papers around on her desk. He looked at her quizzically as he sat down.

"Hey, Maddie. I'm going to jump right into it. I heard about the break-in last night. Your brother called me. How are you holding up?" Davis looked at her as if waiting for her to spill her guts about the event.

Well, she wasn't going to indulge him. "It wasn't great, that's for sure. But no harm no foul. Maybe it was someone who had gotten lost during the gala. Whatever."

She shrugged and Davis raised an eyebrow. Clearly, he wasn't buying what she was selling, but she changed the subject immediately.

"So, as I was leaving the restaurant before the gala last night, I literally ran into Chris Dailey's girlfriend, Ashley. She was a wreck. Upset and crying about Chris and not getting information from the cops on what happened. I guess I have a good listening face because she really opened up to me. I think she just needed to vent and I happened to be in the right place at the right time."

He looked at her and rolled his eyes. "And I'm sure you didn't encourage her at all. Did you find anything out that should go to the police?"

Madeline proceeded to tell him all about the phone call Ashley overheard. Angry phone calls are always suspicious. She then passed the piece of paper with the list of names over to Davis. "This also fell out of her purse and I found it before I left. It seemed interesting. It's pretty much everyone who could be considered a suspect in the murder as far as I can see."

Davis took the list and looked at it thoughtfully.

The list was pretty straightforward:

1. Ben Boucher
2. William Chase
3. Brittany Marks
4. Walter Lawson
5. David Murphy
6. Richard Murphy

Some of the names Madeline knew, but some were unknown. She looked to Davis to see if any of the other names ring any bells for him. The names that surprised her the most, outside of her brother of course, were David Murphy and his father, Richard. What connection could they have with Chris, and was that why he was in our dugout when he was murdered?

She waited as patiently as she could, tapping her fingers rhythmically on her desk. She willed him to read faster. He sat back, staring at a point somewhere behind her head with his brow furrowed. It was a thinking look. She wondered if he had the same questions she did. She didn't have to wait too long to find out.

"Richard Murphy? I know him through his son. Do you know anything else about him?" Davis asked.

She thought for a minute. "No, I don't know all that much about him. Just that he's dedicated to his son's career and he attends every game. Ben might know more since he's been here longer."

She reached over to her phone and typed in his extension. "Ben? Can you come to my office for a minute? Davis and I want to ask you something."

She hung up the phone and sat back behind her desk. A few seconds later Ben strolled into her office with his hands in his pockets. Taking a seat next to Davis, he looked at both of them expectantly. "Is this about the break-in last night?"

Madeline looked sharply at her brother. "We already talked about it, Ben. You had talked to Davis and I just reiterated that there wasn't anything to worry about. I scared the person away and couldn't chase them through the parking lot. Nothing was taken, so again, no big deal."

Davis looked at her, shaking his head. "I still think you need to be more careful, Maddie. With a potential murderer running around who apparently knows their way around the ballpark, you should be more careful when you're alone. And you definitely shouldn't be confronting any burglars."

She waved a hand, "Fine, I know. I'll be more careful next time. Now, can we get back to the list?"

Davis rolled his eyes at her again and handed the list over to Ben. "Ben, do you have any information about Richard Murphy and his son that might help in the investigation? Maddie found this paper and she thinks it might be some sort of suspect list about the murder."

Ben thought for a second and then spoke. "Rich is a great guy. I've known him for a while, ever since David came to the team years ago. He's super supportive of his son, and he's supportive of the team. I've never heard a bad word about him. I find it hard to believe that he'd have anything to do with Chris' murder."

Madeline couldn't decide if she should tell the guys about the fight she witnessed between Tom and Rich. Fight was probably a strong word, she guessed argument was a better term for it. Before she could tell them the story, Davis jumped in and quizzed Ben some more.

"How long has David been with the team?"

Ben put a finger to his chin and thought for a minute. "I think it's been about three full years now. He was one of the first people my Dad signed out of the Cape League. He's a decent player, got an injury during his final games with the league that hindered his pro chances. When we offered him a spot on the team, he and his dad jumped on the opportunity. I guess we were the only team of any caliber interested in him at that point. His father was heavily involved in the negotiation and signing process, but I never felt that he was too pushy."

Madeline pulled up David Murphy's bio on the team website and followed along with Ben's story as he explained it to Davis.

Ben continued, "In fact, I think his mother passed away when he was young, so his father really had to raise him on his own. I know when the pro career didn't work out, his father pushed him into joining the independent league here. Most kids would've given up, but David had a good support system. His dad has been nothing but supportive. I've never heard him say a bad word about his son or the team. Rich wasn't one of those crazy parents who seemed to live life vicariously through his kid. He seemed genuinely happy for his son to have the opportunity to keep playing."

Davis looked at Madeline, urging her with a hand to ask any questions she had. "Other than this list, do you know if either David or his father ever met Chris Dailey or had dealings with him in the scouting world? I find it hard to believe he would have any steroid connections; David seems like such a straight shooter." She looked at her brother.

"That would be something you'd have to talk with the manager about. We don't really get involved in any discipline stuff unless we really have to. First line of defense in making sure our guys are clean is the manager and his staff. If there is an issue, then it comes up our way for further investigation. As of right now, I haven't heard of any of our guys in trouble. Granted, the season has just started, but I think Billy has a good grip on his guys." Ben made to get up and headed towards the door. "Tell you what. I'll head down to the practice field later today to get a sense from Billy if there are any issues that we should be looking out for. Does that work for your guys?"

Ben looked at both Davis and Madeline. She got a sense that he was trusting her on this investigation, even if Davis was bothering her about it. She knew her brother was more worried than he let on about the investigation focusing on him, even if they had moved on.

Before Madeline could respond, Ben looked at Davis and spoke. "So, Davis, any thoughts on the break-in last night? Could it be related to the murder?"

Davis looked at Ben warily and then pierced Madeline with a hard stare. Madeline tried not to meet his eye and cleared her throat. Looking back up at him, she could feel her face turning red in embarrassment. "Look, nothing happened. Just some person rummaging around in Ben's desk." She pointed at the side door. "They ran out that door and took off. I didn't see a car or anything. Maybe it was just a curious partygoer."

Davis shook his head. "C'mon, Maddie. You don't believe that, do you? I wish you wouldn't have tried to investigate in the first place. You should've just called the police as soon as you heard someone in the offices."

"I didn't want to call the police right away if it was just Ben looking for a pen or something in his office. I talked with him about it last night and I realized I was probably overreacting. It was late and I don't think anything really happened, but I'll call Detective Stephenson and let him know about the break-in. Ben, just double check to see if anything is missing in the light of day." Madeline raised her hands in surrender.

After parting ways with the two guys, she settled back in behind her desk to get her actual job done. She was working on a social media day at the ballpark.

Discounted tickets, swag bags, and a chance for a meet and greet with a current player. The season would be in full swing by the time the event rolled around, but she wanted to make sure everything was in order well in advance. She spent the rest of the day working on the logistics and before she knew it, it was quitting time.

Eliza poked her head into the doorway. "Hey girl, you leaving? It's getting late!"

Madeline checked her watch. It was already five-thirty. With no game for the night, she knew she should take this free time while she could. She shut down her computer and lifted a finger up to indicate that Eliza should wait. She wanted to check in with her, see if there was any gossip floating around about the murder.

Okay, now she was feeling weird. Thinking of it as "their" suspect list. She was sure the police were on top of things even if they hadn't made an arrest yet. It had been two weeks. She would've thought something big would've happened by now. Maybe her perspective was skewed from crime shows and detective novels. The suspect was usually caught pretty quickly. Heck, on *Law and Order*, it was always done in the first few days.

The team was lucky there was not a whole lot of media coverage on the murder. All it would take is one person asking questions to bring the attention back to the ballpark and the family. She didn't want that to happen. She would prefer this whole thing be wrapped up quickly.

Madeline followed Eliza out the door. "So, heard any good gossip lately?"

Eliza saw right through her fishing attempt at information. "Girl, are you still trying to solve the murder all on your own? You know that's not your job, right? He was a bad dude. Who knows what kind of people he knew from his days in the joint. Not exactly Club Med there, friend." Eliza shook her head at Madeline as they approached their cars. "But, since you asked so nicely, I did hear a rumor that he was seen around the ballpark more frequently. Plus, my friend Jacinda at the Barnstable stadium said he was hanging around there a lot lately, too. She didn't know why, but he was thrown out by security twice." Eliza winked at her and got into the car.

"Eliza, you're seriously the best." Madeline waved as Eliza pulled her small Mazda out of the parking lot. She lived in Plymouth, which was just over twenty minutes (without traffic) from the stadium. She had grown up out there and loved it. She was married with two young children, but she never let that get in the way of having fun. Her kids were staples at the ballpark during the summer, and her parents loved having them around. Since Madeline and her brother weren't close to providing grandchildren to them in the near future, they liked the excuse to spoil the kids when they could.

It was funny how priorities changed with a new job. With the change in commute and work life, Madeline had much more time to reflect on her life and future. She loved being able to work with her family at a place she loved, but also loved the new amount of free time she had to herself as well. Before coming home, she was constantly on emails, texts, and phone calls.

Of course, she realized the past week was an anomaly. Her time was taken up with the Chris Dailey murder. She knew she should focus on the team and ballpark, but his death haunted her. It might have been because she found the body, or because Ben was a suspect, but she wanted closure on the incident. Shaking herself out of the gloomy thoughts, she pulled into the driveway of her home.

Chapter Eleven

Madeline's home was a typical New England Cape style house. One floor, a few bedrooms, a large bay window for the cats to sit in, small colorful plants framing the walkway, and a set of black shutters framing the windows. She had owned it for about five years, and even though it was small, it was still her space. While only two bedrooms, one room was converted to an office that she used as her space to work from home in. Now, she would probably only use it during the winter off-season or when the team wasn't at the park.

Being social media consultant meant most of her job was spent on the computer and not necessarily in meetings. Only when planning events did she need to meet with other people in the office. She just loved going to the park any chance she got. It felt like a second home. She especially loved being in the office on game days. That's when the excitement really ramped up (especially if the team was on a winning streak). The family usually used game days to come together to do a quick family check. She loved being able to see her mom every day now. When she worked in the city, meetings with the family were pretty sporadic. A dinner here and there and a game when she could duck out. Now they actually had time together.

Grabbing her mail, she let herself in the front door, and greeted her three cats that came running to the door. She knew she fit the stereotype of a crazy cat lady by living alone, not having a boyfriend, and spending weekends with her cats, but she loved them just the same. They were all rescues and living a great life with her. She always made sure to spend time with each cat, ten minutes of cuddling time apiece, making sure they got lots of individual attention. As she snuggled with her eldest cat, she noticed a thin white envelope mixed in with her bills and magazines. It had no return address and only had her name in black Sharpie written across the cover.

She put her other mail down on the side table and cracked open the back seal of the envelope. Inside was a small piece of paper, no bigger than a gum wrapper, with one sentence written on it.

KEEP YOUR NOSE OUT OF OUR BUSINESS — A FRIEND

Well, it if was meant as a threat to her, it worked. Not only was the statement vaguely threatening, the fact that it was left in her mailbox without a stamp or address on it was equally as horrifying. She quickly put on her house alarm, even though it was still early in the evening. She wasn't going to take any chances.

She whipped out her cellphone and quickly typed a text to Davis letting him know what she found. He texted within five seconds a terse "I'll be right there" reply. She carefully picked up the piece of paper by the corners, hoping she wouldn't smudge any fingerprints, if there were any, and grabbed a sandwich bag to put it in. In a separate bag, she placed the envelope. Then, she sat down to wait.

Tapping her leg uncontrollably, she looked towards the clock on her phone and tried to relax. She jumped out of her skin when she heard the knock at the door before realizing it was Davis. He had taken about ten minutes to get there, and she noticed his SUV parked in her driveway as she let him in the house. She saw that she had picked up a baseball bat at the door just in case and placed it back down by the front door for safety purposes. As someone living alone, she tried to take precautions. She turned off the house alarm and opened the door.

"Davis, I'm so glad you're here. The note was a little weird to say the least, and I wasn't sure if it was a police matter, so I called you first." Madeline ushered him through the front hallway.

Looking at the two baggies she had laid out on the kitchen table, Davis looked grim. "I already called Detective Stephenson on the way over. He's going to swing by in an hour to takes these down to the station. Threats should be taken seriously, especially since you were the one who found Chris' body. Although the threat doesn't spell it out exactly, I would bet money it has something to do with all the investigating you've been doing lately."

When she first saw the note, she was freaked out, sure, but not super scared. Cautious, but not terrified. But now that Davis was there, she realized the worst-case scenario of the threat. What if the killer thought she knew more than she did? She didn't even think she knew anything of importance anyway. Other than the list Chris' girlfriend dropped the other night, she didn't even know who the other suspects could be. Her breath caught in her throat as she became a trifle panicked. She was just the social media person, not a detective.

Davis said he would hang around until the detective came. Madeline was not a cook, so she thought ordering a pizza would be the prudent thing to do while they waited. She knew her local pizza joint phone number by heart and that they would get it quickly. When she got nervous, she ate. After ordering her usual cheese pizza, she grabbed two Diet Coke's from the fridge and brought them out to where Davis was sitting in her living room.

"Do you think this threat is serious, Davis? Should I worry about it?" Madeline looked at him.

Davis thought for a minute as he took a sip of the drink. "Honestly, I don't know, Maddie. I would be more careful about who you talk to about this stuff though. The police are investigating, and now it seems like something bigger might be involved. I just want you to be safe." He turned his attention back to the can of soda. He looked as if he might say something else, but apparently changed his mind. 'I just don't know, Maddie. I wonder why they think you're so close to figuring things out. I mean, you haven't done anything I haven't known about, right?"

She shook her head, hoping that she wasn't lying to him. She thought she had told him everything, but the night was so crazy she was worried she was missing something.

"I mean, why would you risk your safety for something out of your control?" He pulled at the tab on the soda can which felt like a nervous habit as he looked at her closely from across the couch.

She wanted him to understand why she couldn't stay out of it. "Davis, it's my family. It's my ballpark. It's my brother, for Pete's sake. The guy was found at my second home; I feel like I need to see it through. Do you get that? I don't mean to put myself in harm's way, but I want to make sure none of this sticks to my family and the team. The baseball team is our life, and I don't want this murder to overshadow the things our family does for the community." At that point, she had jumped up and began pacing the living room. Shaking her head, she still couldn't get past the fact that first there was a murder at the ballpark, second that she was involved, and third that Davis was sitting in her house because a threatening note was sent. This sort of stuff only happened in books and movies.

At the sound of another car pulling into the driveway, she stopped pacing and looked out the front window. Davis also looked up from his can of soda at the sound. Peering from behind the blinds, she saw that Detective Stephenson had hopped out of his car, looked around, and sauntered up her driveway. There was no other way to put it. He sauntered. Not moseying, but sauntering. Like he knew something she didn't and couldn't wait to tell her. He probably did since he was with the police and all. She hoped they knew more than her. They were the ones actually getting paid to get to the bottom of things.

The knock startled her out of her thoughts, even though she knew who it was. She went to the door, and gestured the detective in. "Thanks for coming, Detective. I wasn't sure if this warranted your time, but I'm glad Davis called you. He's already here and I have the note in a baggie just in case you could get fingerprints or evidence or whatever off of it." She ushered him into the living room where Davis had laid out the baggies on the coffee table.

Shaking his head at the offer of a drink, he plunked down in the chair that Madeline had vacated when she answered the door.

"Madeline, have you been looking into this case behind my back?" He had a hint of a smile on his face, but she could hear the rebuke in his tone. "You know you need to leave this to the professionals, right?"

As she turned to find another chair to sit in, she rolled her eyes. "Detective, trust me, I'm not going out of my way to find out what happened. The other night I just happened to run into Chris' girlfriend and she was upset. I couldn't leave her crying at the bar. I don't want her to think ill of my family! For gosh sakes, her boyfriend was just murdered in the family ballpark. If she's that unhappy, who knows what kind of stink she could cause in the press if she felt the family was ignoring her. Then, that piece of paper fell out of her purse. I don't know what it meant so I asked some questions. Before I could get in contact with you again, that note was slipped into my mail."

He sighed at her and sat back in the chair. Looking at Davis for help, the detective turned his focus back to Madeline. "Okay, okay. I get it. You're not actively going out of your way to court trouble. But I definitely need to know if you find out anything else on your own. We do have a list of suspects that closely mirrors that paper you found in Ashley's purse. I'm glad Davis passed it along today because we started clearing some names off of it."

Madeline was struck by another thought and leaned forward. "I told you about the steroids, right? That's got to be a big motive. No team likes to be involved in that kind of thing. I got the sense that Billy was holding back a few swear words as he told me about it earlier."

"Yes, Madeline," he said sighing. "We are looking into that. We have found only one team outside of your family's that was approached by Mr. Dailey regarding a scheme of that nature. Drew Smith from the Foxboro team pointed us in the right direction. Now, before you get excited, that wasn't the team that was approached. We're going to investigate as we see fit." The detective stood up, grabbed the two bags off the table, and made for the front door.

After promising Madeline and Davis to let them know if they found anything, he sauntered back to his car. Davis followed closely behind, but only after reminding Madeline to lock up and get the alarm on. Her vicious watch cats wouldn't be enough to keep out any intruders.

Chapter Twelve

After a fitful night of sleep where Madeline kept dreaming of breaking windows and baseball bat wielding attackers, she woke up before the sunrise and decided to get an early jump on her day. The ballpark was still her favorite place to collect her thoughts, even with all the drama swirling around it.

Davis, Detective Stephenson, and Madeline had discussed precautions the night before. The police added a few extra patrols to her neighborhood and even beefed up some security at the ballpark as well, due to the suspicious behavior. She felt a little guilty about taking up so much time from the police; she was sure they had more important things to do. Then again, she was unnerved that someone threatened her and knew where she lived.

Even though that note threatened her, she was wasn't going to cower in her house all day. She had work to do. After a quick shower, she changed into her work uniform of a black jersey mid-length skirt and blue team polo. There was no game scheduled for that particular day. Early afternoon games were mostly held on weekends. Like most major league teams, there were night games during the week, but most of those were out of town for the Abington team. The town was very strict about having the ballpark lights on at night, so the team tried to schedule most night games later in the week. The team would be heading to Brockton later in the evening for a game, but there was a baseball camp scheduled to visit the park that day so some of the players would be around in the early afternoon to help with the campers. At the start of the season, she let the social media followers of the team know about camping opportunities on the field, behind the scenes ballpark tours, and even batting practice opportunities with the players.

Even with the murder happening fairly recently, she thought they seemed to get through unscathed. It didn't seem to affect people's desire to attend the ballpark, and it didn't seem to bother the day campers and their families either. The week the day campers were scheduled, the team was playing in Barnstable.

Since it was an away game, practices were limited to earlier in the day due to the travel between the two ballparks. It also gave the campers an opportunity to meet more of the players.

Heading into the front office, Madeline saw Eliza already on the phone rolling her eyes at whoever was on the other end of the line.

"No, no, we don't have any comment and would ask that you please direct your questions to the proper authorities. Thank you! Have a nice day!" she said with forced cheerfulness as she hung up the phone without waiting for more of a response. Waving Madeline over, she heaved an exasperated sigh and give her a look.

"Girl, that was your friend, the reporter. She's trying to pump us for more information about Ben and Chris Dailey's relationship. I made sure not to tell her anything, but she was awfully persistent. I hope she doesn't try to cause any trouble to you or the family." Eliza shook her head.

Madeline sighed and closed her eyes. "Thanks for the heads up, Eliza. If she calls again, just send her to my phone. I want to find out what she's digging for." Madeline wanted to know why Jennifer Roberts was so involved with the case. She understood it was the reporter's job to be a journalist and look for a story, but Madeline thought she was focused in the wrong direction. Her brother was already cleared according to Davis anyway, so what else was the reporter looking for?

Madeline set her purse down in the office, quickly checked her email, and looked to see if she had any voicemails. The first was from the day camp that was arriving that day making sure they had the correct start time. The second was from an unidentified number with no talking, just heavy breathing. Normally, she would just chalk that up to an errant butt dial, but after all the weirdness with the murder, she was instantly suspicious. Checking her watch, she realized she only had ten minutes before the campers arrived for their day at the field. She wanted to make sure Davis knew about the voicemail though, just in case it was something nefarious.

She dashed down the hallway to Davis' office. For the first time since she could remember he wasn't sitting at his desk before she went into his office. He was always the first person in the office, almost as if he slept there sometimes. She scoured his desk for some paper and a pen. Madeline quickly scribbled a note about the weird call and stuck it to his computer monitor with a piece of tape. Hopefully he would be able to trace the call or something to figure out if the call was just creepy or threatening.

Rushing down the ramp to the field, she found the team meeting in their home dugout, probably getting a quick pep talk about the next game. Not wanting to interrupt, she backtracked up the ramp to the front entrance to the park. She shielded her eyes from the sun as she looked over the parking lot. The school bus carrying the kids from the camp pulled up at the front door and began unloading about twenty kids and four adults. Luckily this group was pretty small since it was an elite summer baseball camp, so the numbers weren't excessive. That meant all the kids could bat and play catch on the field with minimum disruption.

Madeline hoped they were well-behaved kids. Aged about 10–13, they should know how to act, but one never knew when it came to pre-teen kids. As much as she didn't love kids, seeing them experience the ballpark for the first time was special to her. She could remember the feelings she had when her Grandpa took her to Fenway Park the first time and she hoped that these kids would feel the same.

She greeted the four adults at the front entrance and shook their hands. Introducing herself as the team representative, she gave them a rundown of the camper's schedule for the day. She ushered the group into the box office area.

Madeline took a look at the group of kids in their baseball uniforms holding well-worn gloves. "Who here is a Red Sox fan?"

A majority of the kids raised their hands. The only two hold outs stood in the back with their arms crossed and wearing New York Yankee hats. So, mostly Red Sox fans, just a few fans of the evil empire. "Well, even those that aren't, this is where most baseball careers begin and end. How many of you have been to a game here at the stadium before?" Every kid and adult raised their hands. "Great! Today is going to be super special then. To start, we're going to take you behind the scenes through the owner's area, the press area, food prep areas, visitors' locker room, and finally the home team locker room. Once down there, we'll be meeting with several members of the coaching team who will show you scouting videos of our players and explain the mechanics of what they do. After lunch, we'll take the field and you get to show us what you got! How does that sound?"

The kids let out a raucous cheer and jumped up and down smacking their gloves. This group was going to be fun. Madeline led the group down the concourse to the family group of offices. Eliza gave the kids a big wave and then buzzed Ben to come out and greet them. Ben came out of his office in similar team attire to Madeline and gave the kids a big hello.

One of the kids in the Yankees hat looked supremely unimpressed at this. Before her brother could lead the kids out on the next part of the tour, the young girl's hand shot into the air.

"Yes, young lady?" Ben asked.

"Are you the guy that killed the other guy on the field? My mom said you got away with it because you're rich." The kid smugly crossed her arms as she finished her question.

Madeline froze and looked towards her brother with horror in her eyes. The coach of the kid's team, who until that time had not much to do, quickly grabbed the girl's hand and pulled her back to a quiet corner of the concourse.

Ben seemed to take the question in stride and quickly changed the subject with the kids.

"Okay, how about we start heading out on the tour now!" Ben started walking out on the concourse towards the press area. The young lady and coach seemed to reach some sort of agreement and followed the group. Madeline pulled one of the other parents to the side as they made their way to the small press door.

"Hey, who is that young lady?"

The father shook his head. "Ya know that reporter lady? Blonde, short skirts, ya know? She's been telling all the other parents how Ben is a murderer and she was going to prove it or something. That's her daughter. But don't worry, none of us believe her. If we did, we wouldn't be here now, would we?" He kept walking, following the team through the door into the press room.

Madeline stopped where she was to process the information. Now things were getting weird. That reporter, Jennifer Roberts, was telling lies and spreading falsehoods about the family, and Madeline was not too happy about that. She needed to call her and get this straightened out sooner rather than later. Plus, Davis needed to know about this girl and her mother. It had been at least 45 minutes since she had left the note on his desk and he still hadn't responded. He knew he could find her anywhere in the park. She hoped nothing serious had happened to him. She resolved to try and ferret him out if she didn't hear from him by lunch time. Maybe he just decided to take the day off. Even security personnel were allowed those days.

Madeline caught up with her brother and the kids in the limited press box. There was one intern for the local paper there working on updating stats, and usually there was only one or two other guys there doing the games themselves. They led the kids down through the concession areas. Since there wasn't a home game that upcoming weekend, everything was empty and cleaned. The visitor's locker room was the same. When the visiting team departed after the game, the team had a crack cleaning team that got it into ship shape before the next morning. The home team locker room was a different story.

Separated into two parts, the first part of the room was the film area. Set up with folding chairs and benches, this was where the players came during practice, before games, and after games to watch tape of previous performances or scout out the next team they would face. This was also the room that interviews after games tended to happen in. The team didn't let anyone into the main locker room for privacy's sake. The second half of the room was behind two more double doors and the kids were led there first.

The locker room proper was where the players had their little cubbies with uniforms and personal products. The players were still out on the field for practice and meetings, so the kids were told they would come back after lunch so they could meet some of the players. They were visibly excited about the prospect, except for the reporter's daughter. She still stood with her arms crossed and a sour look on her face.

Madeline rolled her eyes and ushered everyone back into the video room and had them take seats. She went back to the coach's office and asked the bench coach, Jason, to come out and give the kids an overview of the scouting process. He introduced himself to the kids and began his speech. Madeline left the kids and Ben in Jason's capable hands and made her way back to the field.

Watching from the sidelines, she found the team finishing up some stretching drills. She waved the manager over and gave him a quick update on what the kids were doing and how the schedule would unfold the rest of the day.

"Everything going okay today? The kids are with Jason now going over some game DVD's. After that, we're going to bring lunch to them in the conference room by the press box. About twelve-thirty, we'll bring them down here to meet the guys for some team drills. Does that work with your schedule today?"

"That sounds great, Maddie." Billy said. "The guys are really excited to work with the kids on drills this afternoon. I'll tell them to take a break now to make sure they're back around twelve to start."

Madeline agreed and quickly headed back to the front offices in hopes that she could catch Davis. She waved at Eliza, who was on the phone, and checked in his office again. His office was empty, and her note was still taped to the screen.

As she moved back into her office, she sank down heavily in her guest chair and shut her eyes. The past few weeks had been a blur of activity. Losing her job, starting a job here, and of course, the murder. Oh, and the baseball season starting in earnest. She needed a few weeks to catch up on her sleep. It didn't seem like it was going to happen anytime soon, especially with that reporter breathing down her family's neck. She hoped the murderer would be caught soon so that she could go back to normal busy things.

She sat back and focused on her emails. Before she knew it, it was time to head back down to lead the kids to lunch in the fancy conference room overlooking the field. It was really just a glorified break room with about thirty chairs and some vending machines. She made her way down towards the locker room and heard a voice from across the concourse. It was coming from one of the little janitorial rooms near the locker area. Part of her wanted to keep walking, but the other, more curious side of her won out as she crept closer to the door. She could only hear one side of the conversation, but it didn't sound pleasant.

"I know! I'll get the money as soon as I can." She heard a man's voice speaking urgently into what she assumed was a phone.

After a beat of silence, she heard the guy continue. "Look, Chris' death was an unforeseen mishap. Give me twenty-four hours and we'll get things back on track."

Another pause.

"Yeah, you too. Bye."

Madeline scampered away from the door and hid in one of the other doorways near the locker room. She heard the janitor close the door and she pulled her cell phone out of her pocket. She didn't want the person to see her, so she turned the phone's camera to selfie mode and tried to see who came out of the door. She pretended to take a picture of herself, even though she hoped the guy didn't notice her at all. She clicked the camera and hoped the guy would be in the background of her selfie.

From the distance she was at, she could only tell it was a tall guy with dark brown hair. He was wearing workout clothes, so maybe even a player? She was annoyed that she couldn't see anything else as the guy walked further away from her hiding place. Just in case, she made sure to snap a picture of his retreating back.

Saving the photo in her phone, she continued into the video part of the locker room. The kids were still listening with rapt attention to Jason as he demonstrated how the pitcher throws a knuckleball. Not many pitchers in the modern game threw the difficult pitch, and catchers definitely don't love to try and catch the wily pitch. Jason caught her eye and gave a little nod. He looked back at the kids and clapped his hands.

"Okay, guys, it looks like you're going to be heading to lunch now. I'll see you guys on the field in about an hour to get some drills in." Jason waved and went back towards his office.

Madeline guided the kids and adults back upstairs to the concourse and finally the conference room. There the team had put out a spread of hot dogs, hamburgers, and sandwiches. Most of the kids went immediately for the hot dogs, so Madeline grabbed a cold sandwich and Diet Coke. Heading towards the field view windows, Madeline sat down with the coaches and parents who were chaperoning the field trip. They were all fairly young, most in their late forties/early fifties, so she felt comfortable talking with them even though she didn't have children.

The father she was talking to earlier leaned over. "Ya, I have a question for you." He smiled and continued. "My son is just starting out with this baseball thing and would love to learn more about the inside of the baseball business, not just the athletic part. He's big into the fantasy sports and thinks that by learning the business of the game he might get better at determining his fantasy roster. Do you offer classes or internships for when they're older that might help guide him?"

Madeline looked over at the other parents who obviously overheard the question and were nodding in agreement. "Well, to be honest, we've never really thought about it before, but it sounds like a great idea for the kids and adults alike. Fantasy is such a big thing now, maybe it would be beneficial to get tips from scouts and front office people. Thanks for the suggestion. Make sure you leave me your information at the front before you leave and I'll keep you posted on what we decide."

He nodded at her and turned back to the other parents. They were all talking about how excited the kids were doing this field trip. "You know, in the summer, it's hard to get them to work on baseball practice. Bringing them here made them that much more excited about the sport. Meeting the players they watch on the field is exciting. I know they'll be talking about this trip for a while." The coach smiled at the players scarfing hot dogs down.

Madeline smiled. "I'm glad. I've been a fan since I was a kid, and I know coming out here to the ballpark and being on the field is a special experience. I'm glad we've started this program again with the day camps and baseball groups. It's nice to have the kids on the field with the players. I know the players like it too. They've been talking about it all week!"

The parents nodded and continued their lunch. Some of them asked questions about the upcoming season, and she tried to answer them as best she could. Since the season had just started, not everything was set in stone schedule wise. The team was lucky to play in a pretty competitive independent league, so the playoffs were never a forgone conclusion. That made every game important.

As the kids finished up their lunch, there was a quick clean up before leading the kids down to the field. After a quick bathroom pit-stop, the kids couldn't keep their feet still when they made it out to the field. While they were taking the tour, the team had unloaded their baseball bags from the bus and left them on the field. As the kids dug through for their gear, trying to find their beloved bats and gloves, Billy and David Murphy came over to greet her and the kids.

"Hey guys, welcome to the park! You ready to play some baseball?" The kids led up a resounding cheer. "Okay, pitchers line up on my left, infield and outfield on my right." Billy pointed in each direction as the kids scrambled to their proper locations.

"Pitchers, you guys will go with David here to work with the bullpen guys. All the rest of ya's can come with me and we'll start working on our outfield and infield drills." The two groups separated and headed to their respective locations. With the kids down on the field being watched by the team, Madeline pulled her phone out of her pocket and went to sit in the shady part of the dugout.

While she sat in the dugout with her feet pulled up next to her, she watched the kids run drills with the team. She used the phone app to take a few pictures to post on the team website and social media. Before any camp sign up for the program, she made sure the parents were aware that she could use the pictures of their kids for marketing purposes on the team's social media accounts. She thought that covered any liability the team had, and so far, there hadn't been any complaints that she knew about. So, she hoped that meant the program would keep going, and use the good publicity for the team benefit, too. Plus, the kids were super adorable when out working with the team.

Madeline had forwarded all her work emails to her phone, so she never missed anything when she was wandering the field and ballpark. She scrolled through her emails and found four emails asking her for a comment regarding some news report from that morning. She hadn't seen anything, so she did a quick search to find out what was happening. On one of the local Boston sites, she found a link that mentioned local murder and baseball club. She clicked the link and turned the volume on her phone up.

After a brief ad for cleaning supplies, she heard the local news anchor's voice. "And finally tonight, we bring you a story we told you about a few weeks ago. Local Christopher Dailey was found murdered in the Abington Armadillos ballpark two weeks ago today. So far, the authorities say there is no connection to anyone on the Abington team, but sources close to the baseball leagues say an investigation into Dailey's illegal activities may be involving one or more of the

Abington organization. While we wait for comment from the team, for now it seems as if this case is far from over."

Madeline ended the video. What do they mean, someone involved with the organization? Player? Coach? Front office member? So, the victim was a bad scout, a drug dealer, and a gambler. Definitely not characteristics of anyone she knew was involved with the team. Of course, she hadn't' been around nearly as much, but she was determined not to let this incident become the team's legacy.

She huffed to herself. She looked back to the field and saw the kids running bunting drills down the third base line. They were scheduled to be on the field for at least two more hours, so she quickly ran back to the offices to see if Davis had returned yet. As she rushed through the concourse, she pulled up her internet search engine to find different news stories about the murder. Not looking where she was going, she ran smack dab into a solid chest. Looking up, she realized it was Davis. "There you are!"

Chapter Thirteen

"Davis! Where have you been? I've been trying to get in touch with you all day!" Madeline pulled him into a hug, startling herself and Davis a bit. "After the last few days I got nervous when you weren't here first thing this morning like usual. I left a note on your computer." She babbled and backed away from Davis as she wrung her hands together. She felt so embarrassed about the random hug and could feel her face redden and felt a hot flash along with it. She took a deep breath and tried to calm her racing heart down.

Davis looked down and tried to not make eye contact with Madeline, sensing her uncomfortableness. He shook his head as if to clear it. "We have to stop meeting like this. Sorry I didn't tell you I would be late today. I had an appointment with this guy this morning that I couldn't get out of. Has something else happened?"

She told him about the reporter stirring up drama on the news and her daughter asking if her brother was a murderer earlier that day. She showed him the news report on her phone and intimated that there was some shady illegal stuff happening with the team. Davis looked thoughtful as he watched the video. He gestured towards the field and guided her to the seats in the grandstand.

"The guy I was meeting with this morning was an old friend of Chris Dailey's." Davis said, putting air quotes around the word friend. "He did some time with Chris for gambling back in the day and had quite a few interesting things to say about the guy."

"Do you think he's a suspect?" Madeline leaned forward excitedly.

"Nah. He just got out of prison a week ago, so he has a pretty solid alibi for the murder."

"Couldn't he have hired someone to off Dailey while in the joint?" She cringed as she heard her use of such weird language. Why didn't she just say prison?

Davis laughed. "I mean, it's possible, but it just seems unlikely. I still think the person who did this had a more personal reason. You don't just go around beating people with a bat unless you really mean it. Also, since the bat was left in the dugout, it's possible this was a crime of passion or opportunity. Maybe the person didn't go there meaning to kill Chris but got mad at something and just started swinging." He turned in the ballpark seat and looked at her quizzically. "Wait a minute, are you still asking questions about this murder? Didn't that note scare you into not wanting to be involved anymore?"

She looked out towards the field and the players running drills. She wondered how she could make him understand her need to get this whole thing resolved. "Yes and no. The note was definitely scary. But too many people are still spreading rumors that my family and my team is behind this murder. That's just not true. So, my fear of the note does not outweigh how important my family is." She shrugged and looked back at Davis who was looking at her thoughtfully.

"Well, I might as well tell you what I told Detective Stephenson since you'll somehow find out anyway. The guy I met with said that Chris was heavily involved in some sort of prison gambling and steroid ring. He wasn't sure how it worked, but basically Chris fancied himself a bookie even behind bars. He kept extensive connections on the outside and seemed to fall back into them when he was released a few years ago. The steroid thing was a bit weirder. One of his outside guys somehow smuggled them in and he facilitated the use by other prisoners. Now, with the scouting, he considered himself an independent contractor so he wouldn't have to follow any particular scouting conventions. For some reason people still met with him even though it seemed shady from the jump." Davis ticked off Chris' various criminal activities on his hand.

Something stuck with Madeline. "That bothers me. This is such a tight knit baseball community. Why would anyone take a flyer on this guy as a scout when we already have a relationship with legitimate scouts that we've all worked with through the years? Most owners I know wouldn't just take the word of a guy they didn't do an extensive check on. Heck, I found out about his shady past in about five minutes doing an online search!"

She shook her head. "Wait, did someone vouch for him to get access to all the teams? That'd be the only way he could get into the circle of scouts."

"I asked the guy that, he wasn't sure. He just knew the guy had some sort of connections to baseball on the outside." Tapping his chin, Davis mused. "I wonder if we could find out though. You said you were introduced to Tom, the scout, right?"

Madeline sat up straighter in the chair. Did Davis know that her Mom was setting her up with Tom? Why else would he randomly bring up his name?

"Ummmm, yea, I met him at the Opening Day gala. Why?"

"Why don't you get in touch with him and ask if he knows how Chris got involved in the scouting world? The only thing I could find out is that Chris first worked with the Barnstable Barnstormers about six months ago. Before that, I have no idea. I would ask the owner, William, but he doesn't seem like the most reliable person, and I wouldn't want to ruffle any feathers or cause more trouble for your family," he said.

Unreliable was the nice way of putting it. The owner of the Barnstormers was a notorious drunk who spoiled events everywhere he went. Madeline remembered how drunk he was getting at the concession party a few weeks prior. Definitely not a good look for an owner of a team. While not working for a major league franchise, the team owners represented their local community. They were supposed to be put together and represent their teams as professionally as possible.

The Boucher family, for example, teamed up with local South Shore schools to provide the summer camp program, and during the school year (the team's offseason), the field was open for kids to come in the afternoon and play in. During the holidays, the team sponsored local charities and even provided warm meals for local homeless. She tried to think of things the Barnstable team did outside of baseball, but was coming up blank.

William Chase was known as the "bad boy" of baseball. He never got really close with any of the other team owners. As far as Madeline knew, William didn't have any friends in the baseball world. That's why it was so weird that he bought a baseball team. A man without connections rarely made it far in this business. She thought he lucked out at the time when the Barnstable team was ready to sell. They lived in the same town as the Cape Cod Baseball League, so they were in a prime position to recruit players when that season came to a close. She wondered why he chose to use Chris Dailey as a scout when the team probably had their own scouts in the system. Maybe she could grill one of the Barnstormer scouts about the relationship between Chris and the owner.

Davis and Madeline agreed that she'd pump Tom for some information as soon as she could. Madeline thought that Davis didn't need to know that she found Tom super cute or that her mother was trying to set her up on a date. Madeline wasn't sure if Davis would care that she was going out with another guy, but she wanted to be able to keep her options open with him just in case.

For now though, she still had to figure out what happened to Chris Dailey. That would be the only way to move on this season without any distractions. Davis got up from the stands while she whipped out her cellphone to dialup Tom. Before she could do that, she realized that even though they made tentative plans, they didn't exchange numbers. She knew the person she needed to call who had the inside track on everyone involved with the team.

She sent a quick text over to Eliza in the office. "Hey, can you get me Tom Baker's phone number? He's the local scout we use for the team."

Almost immediately a response came back. "Of course! I knew you couldn't resist him," followed by his number, a heart emoji, and a kissy face emoji. Madeline sighed, knowing that the gossip mill would be churning now.

She pushed the number for it to go through as a telephone call. She took a deep breath and sighed in relief when after five rings it went to voicemail. Much easier to leave a message.

"Hi, you've reached Tom Baker. I can't get to my phone right now, but if you leave your name and number, I'll get back to you as soon as I can." *Beep.*

Madeline took a deep breath right before the beep. "Hey, Tom, it's Madeline from the Abington Armadillos. We spoke at the gala the other night. I hope things are going well. I was wondering if you could give me a call back as soon as you get a chance. I'm working on a project over here and have some questions that you could possibly answer." She rattled off her cell phone number and hung up.

She looked out at the field with the kids running the bases. They had lucked out with a beautiful day. The kids looked like they were having a great time and even the chaperones were getting into it by fielding fly balls and swinging for the fences. She checked her watch and saw that there was about an hour left before the bus came to pick the kids up. She decided to take one more trip to the office to see if there was anything that needed to be done before the end of the day.

Before she could make it to her office, Eliza stopped her in the waiting area." Hey, girl, your mom is in her office and asked me to grab you as you went by. Don't worry, I didn't tell her about you looking for Tom's number." She gave Madeline a conspiratorial wink as she made her way back behind the desk.

Madeline rolled her eyes and gave Eliza the okay sign. She knocked on her Mom's office door and went in. She gestured at the chair opposite her desk and Madeline sat down. "Maddie, we need to talk, sweetie. Ben has been telling me that you're investigating that death here at the park. Do you think that's wise? Your father and I have talked about it and we want to make sure you both stay safe. Let the police do their job and we can go from there. So far we've weathered this storm pretty well."

Madeline changed the subject so she wouldn't have to lie to her mom about continuing to ask questions. "Did you see the latest news report? Someone forwarded it to me earlier." Her mother shook her head. Madeline queued up the video and let her Mom watch it before continuing.

"I believe that girl Jennifer is spreading the rumors about the team to get a better story. Now they're saying something shady was going on behind the scenes with the team. That bothers me so much. It's bad enough we're trying to clear up this murder thing, but now they're insinuating drug use and gambling? Oh, and catch this. Jennifer's daughter is one of the kids at the day camp today and accused Ben of being a murderer in front of everyone." Madeline shook her head. "I'm not actually investigating, Mom, just asking some questions."

Madeline decided not to reveal the weird phone call or threatening note that she got to her mother. There wasn't any need to worry her since it wasn't probably that serious. She had Davis to help her on that end. She also wasn't going to tell her about meeting up with Tom to get more information about scouting and the Barnstable team.

For some reason, that team was pinging Madeline's intuition. She had a feeling that the key to everything might involve that team and their owner. Whether that meant the team owner or players on the team she wasn't sure, but she was determined to find out. William Chase was the key she was sure of it. He was acting weird at that party, and then he accosted her at the game. He either knew something or was just supremely creepy. Or both. He could definitely be both.

Before she left her mom's office, she thought of something that she should check. "By the way, did William Chase ever set up a meeting with Dad? He stopped me on Opening Day to talk about a partnership or something like that."

Her mom thought for a moment, drumming her fingers on the desktop. "I don't believe so. That's something your father definitely would've told me about. We never really partnered with another team outside of the Foxboro team. And the only reason we do that is because of the relationship we have with that family, and the tradition of playing them on Opening Day. Barnstable is too new and too close to our market to want to partner with. Plus, I don't like that William guy. He gives me the willies." She shivered behind her desk.

"No argument from me, Mom. I feel the same way." Madeline left her office and made her way to her own desk.

She had about 20 minutes before the camp wrapped up, which was just enough time to check her emails and social media accounts. Nothing crazy immediately jumped out at her on the public team sites. There were a few people asking if the investigation was ongoing at the park, but nobody outright accusing the family of being responsible in any way for the death. She clicked over to her email after uploading some pictures of the team practicing with the kids from that day.

She had about thirteen emails, all with variations of the same subject from one particular email address. It was an unfamiliar address to her, which sounded off alarms in her head. The subject lines of the emails were all variations of her brother's name and the victim's name. In each email, it said "Your brother did it. You know it and I know it. It's only a matter of time before the police know it." After confirming that yes, all thirteen emails said the same thing, she zipped them in a file and sent it over to Davis via the office email system. Before she even exited out of the system, Davis was in her office.

"Again? Okay, now things are getting weird. I'm going to talk to some IT folks I know and see if they can do any trace on this email address." He shook his head and grabbed a piece of paper off her desk. "We're going to figure out who is doing this and why. We're also going to make sure the police are made aware of these threats as well. 'Cause that's definitely what they are. Threats or at the very least, harassment." He scribbled down the email address and the timeline of all the emails. It looked like the first email was sent while Madeline was out with the kids getting the tour going.

Davis and Madeline made plans to meet up at Centerfields after she got the kids back to their bus and Davis had time to work on his connections to see if they could figure anything else out. She closed out of her computer, grabbed her cell phone, and headed back to the field. The kids were just finishing up and the players were signing some autographs on the kid's bats and gloves. Each kid had a wide smile and the players themselves all seemed in high spirits.

Madeline waved at the coach of the kid's team and gestured them towards the ballpark exit where the bus was waiting. They quickly rounded up the kids and headed that way. She waved to the manager and the players, reminding herself to thank them later for all they did that day. The team was special for sure. After all her hesitation, she was really starting to enjoy working with everyone in the organization. Of course, the murder put a damper on everything, but the day-to-day stuff was wearing down her defenses.

The kids boarded their bus and yelled a big thank you to Madeline and the staff hanging around. The staff all waved until the bus was out of sight and

Madeline checked her watch. Only 4 p.m. She still had time to do a quick walk around the ballpark before meeting Davis at the restaurant. The next game wasn't until the next weekend, so everything was pretty closed up for the day. The concession people wouldn't come in until two days before the game to set up all their necessary equipment. On game day, they showed up about six hours early to make sure things were prepared. Gates opened two hours before game time, and that's when most people got their snacks, drinks, and souvenirs.

She made her way back to the field and saw the team having one more meeting before Billy dismissed them for the day. She decided to head to the restaurant and wait for Davis there. On the way back to the office to grab her purse, she felt her phone vibrate in her pocket. Pulling it out, she found a text message from Tom. Short, sweet, and to the point, it said "Meet me at Centerfields at 6. I'm free then and we can chat."

Putting the phone back in her pocket, she stopped before grabbing her purse. She wondered if she was using Tom for just his scouting knowledge or if it was going to be something like a date tonight. He was cute, and she would like to go out with him, but she wasn't sure where his head was at. Plus, there was Davis to think about, too. Well, hopefully she could get some good information out of him that night and they could see where they would go from there.

Chapter Fourteen

Madeline walked into the restaurant and her stomach tightened anxiously. It was just going to be her and Davis having drinks together. Alone. Like a date. She told herself it was strictly professional. He's just meeting with her as head of security for the team. Trying to solve a murder, talking gambling and steroids. Not exactly hot first date talk. Even still, she took a moment at the front door to tuck her hair behind her ears and smooth down the front of her shirt. She wanted to make sure everything looked put together before she saw Davis.

She let her eyes adjust to the darkness of the sports bar and scanned the crowd to see if Davis had made it yet. She looked around and noticed William Chase at the bar, talking to Ashley, the victim's girlfriend. They had their heads bent close together, and there were several empty glasses in front of them. They appeared to be having a heated conversation and had probably been at the bar for several hours. To quote Lewis Carroll, "curiouser and curiouser."

Madeline turned as she heard her name called from behind her. At the sound of her name, both William and Ashley looked up and caught her staring at them. She gave them a jaunty wave and a big smile so they wouldn't think she was staring at them but just being friendly. They looked at each other and then waved back nervously before scooting away from each other at the bar. Ashley picked up her beer glass and headed towards the pool tables. Madeline wondered why they were pretending not to be friends since they had looked so close before.

Madeline turned around and found Davis entering the restaurant behind her. He had changed from the suit she had seen him in earlier to a more casual outfit of khaki shorts and a blue button-down shirt. She looked down at her work outfit and cringed. She should've taken the time to change into something a bit more presentable. Of course, he looked good and she looked a mess. They let the hostess lead them to a table in the back where it was less crowded and they could talk without screaming at each other.

She gave him a quick rundown of seeing William and Ashley at the bar. She didn't even know that they had known each other, but I guess Chris was the common ground between the two of them. She still didn't know how William knew and vouched for Dailey, but she was determined to find out. Davis seemed intrigued by the idea of the Chris connection between the two, but if he had formulated any ideas, he was not making her privy to his thoughts. Instead he just nodded his head and tried to look over to the bar to catch a glimpse of the two of them.

The waitress appeared shortly after that and Madeline remembered that she was meeting Tom that night, too. "Davis! I forgot to tell you. Tom's coming at six and I want to make sure I asked about the connection between Dailey and Chase. It's definitely something interesting now that I saw Chase talking to Dailey's girlfriend in such a compromising situation." She sat back satisfied.

Davis smiled, not giving away any of his feelings about her meeting Tom. "Only you, Maddie. They were hardly in a compromising position. They were sitting at a bar talking. It's a little bit loud up front there, maybe he just leaned in to hear her better. You always look for the drama in everything."

Before Madeline could respond, the waitress plopped two plates of burgers and fries in front of them. Madeline contented herself with rolling her eyes at Davis and instead turned her focus to her delicious burger. She hadn't eaten since lunch with the kids and she was starving. The whole investigation thing was making her hungrier than normal. She wasn't one of those of girls who watched what they ate in front of cute guys, and she had a tendency to eat her feelings when stressed. In fact, if she was more stressed out than normal she could eat her weight in french fries. And her waistline was proof of that.

Chewing in silence for a little while, she broke the quiet by almost choking on a piece of french fry. Coughing, she discreetly pointed at the front door. Davis turned his head. Walking in the restaurant was Jennifer, the news reporter that had been hounding her family for the past two weeks. Madeline tried ducking behind the drinks on the table, but apparently it didn't work. She heard a set of high heels clacking across the floor and stopping in front of their table.

"Well, well, well. Isn't this cozy?" Jennifer said, tapping her foot at the end of the table. "I've been trying to get in touch with you for a comment and here you are schmoozing with the head of security. That's interesting."

Madeline rolled her eyes. "Jennifer, I'm hardly schmoozing as you so eloquently put it. I'm having dinner with a co-worker before heading home for the night. And you're right. I have gotten your messages, but we just don't have any comment regarding the murder. You need to talk to the police. I told you that last time you bothered me."

Jennifer huffed a loud sigh and folded her arms across her chest. "Whatever. I'm just trying to give the public what they want. If you don't give me info, I'll have to go somewhere else then to get the scoop." She flounced away. Madeline couldn't think of a better way to describe it. Jennifer's ponytail swished behind her as the heels tapped a staccato rhythm across the floor.

"What do you think she means by that?" Madeline said to Davis, grimacing. "Wait, she's now talking to William!"

Jennifer stopped at William's bar stool and started talking in a very animated fashion to the man sitting there. She was flailing her arms and pointed back at the table Davis and Madeline were sitting at.

"That can't be good," Madeline said.

Before she could get up and confront the two and see what was going on, William slammed his hand down on the bar counter, stood up, threw a bunch of money down, and stormed out while Jennifer looked on in astonishment. The woman didn't seem to know what to do and Jennifer just turned and walked out the door behind him.

At that exact moment, Tom walked in the door of the restaurant. Madeline quickly wiped her face to make sure all the ketchup evidence was taken care of and grabbed her purse. Davis shook his head, also noticing Tom come in.

"I got it this time, Maddie. Just make sure you remember to tell me everything you find out."

Thanking him, she got up and greeted Tom at the door. He looked like he just got out of a business meeting, wearing a suit and tie.

"Ah, you didn't have to get dressed up for this," she teased.

Tom sort of blushed and looked down at his clothes. "I know it's not the most appropriate attire for a sports bar, but I had a meeting that ran long this afternoon at the club and didn't have time to change."

In addition to being a scout for local baseball teams, Tom was also a successful health club owner on the South Shore. He had two gyms in the local area and she had heard he was looking to expand as far as Boston. Madeline liked that he had multiple interests and seemed to be comfortable in his life.

"Do you want to get a drink?"

He guided Madeline to the bar with his hand on her lower back. They moved to the opposite side of the bar from Ashley and the men at the pool tables. Madeline noticed Ashley taking sneaky looks as the two of them sat down. As

Madeline made eye contact with her, she quickly turned away and rummaged around in her purse. She threw some money down and hightailed it out of the bar.

Madeline looked back at Tom as they got settled on the bar stools, but he didn't seem to notice Ashley at all. Maybe he'd never met her before. It sure seemed like she had her eyes on Tom from the moment he entered the bar, but then again maybe that's because he's so good looking. She shook her head to clear her thoughts and bring her mind back to the task at hand. This was about the murder. Not the cute guy.

"Thanks for coming to meet me tonight, Tom. I know it sort of came from out of the blue." She smiled at him.

He smiled back. "No problem. What is it you wanted to ask me? Is it about Chris Dailey's murder?"

"Wait, how did you know?" Madeline sat up straight.

He waved his hands in a calm down gesture. "Whoa, I've just heard rumors that you're looking into it."

Madeline sagged in her seat. "Oh, it's just been a weird time and I wasn't sure who knew what. I wasn't only asking you out to talk about murder. I mean, not that this is a date. I mean, it could be, but it's also professional. Ah, you know what I mean."

Tom laughed and put Madeline at ease right away. "This doesn't have to be a date. That can come later. For now, we can talk about murder."

Madeline put her head in her hand in embarrassment. "Oh, okay. Technically I don't want to talk about the murder. I want to know about the person. I heard he wasn't too savory of a character and was possibly into illegal drugs and stuff like that. I thought maybe you'd have some background on him from being involved in the scouting world." She leaned closer to him in order to hear his answer over the noise of the bar.

He thought for a minute, tapping his fingers on the bar counter. "You know, I didn't know him all that well. I've heard the rumors too, of course. I think it was something mainly going on with the Barnstable team. You know they had a couple of guys kicked out of the league for dealing drugs, right?"

Madeline shook her head. It seemed she was just scratching the surface with these guys and the steroid epidemic. She was worried it was more than just the Barnstable team. She didn't know how many other teams in the league were involved. Steroids are usually thought of as a major league problem, not so much in the lower leagues. Of course, it was probably a problem anywhere there were athletes looking for any advantage they could.

Tom shook his head, interrupting Madeline's thoughts. "It's pretty bad actually in the lower leagues. You get a bunch of guys who may have had a shot, but for whatever reasons don't make it to the bigger stage. They want to get bigger, stronger, faster, and hope that they can make it out to a big squad eventually. You tend to find it in the players who were injured during their career, or someone who is a bit older than the other guys. The college kids tend to be less of steroid fans, but that changes sometimes if they get injured. They just want to keep playing."

"That's terrible. And sad." Madeline said. "How do they get the drugs in this area? Was Chris known as a supplier to the teams? How exactly did he get into the baseball business after his prison stint? It doesn't seem he was well liked by anyone around here."

Tom spread his arms out. "Honestly, I don't know. I just know that one day I went out to the Barnstable field to check out some recruits I had scouted when Dailey came up and introduced himself. He said he was another scout hired by William Chase to check out some recruits from outside the district. I thought it was a little weird that William hired him personally. Most of us scouts are independent of teams for a reason. That way there is no favoritism played to certain owners and teams."

Nodding, Madeline said, "That makes sense. So, I wonder why William did that. Not only did he hire a former felon, he hired one that had no scouting experience, and from what I hear, no baseball experience at all."

Tom agreed. "You're right, it's totally weird. Now, I don't know the actual reason he was hired, but I can tell you one of the rumors going around. The rumor is that William Chase got into some kind of trouble that Chris Dailey was blackmailing him for. I never heard what kind of trouble it was, but if Chris was involved it would make sense that the problem could be gambling. I don't know William all that well, and he hasn't really cultivated a relationship with any other scouts, so he's a bit hard to read."

"Blackmail though?" She said. "That seems so weird. That doesn't happen to normal people, does it? Of course, I thought murder didn't happen to normal people either. Yet, here we are, or here my family is, stuck in this mess." Madeline sighed and sipped her glass of Pinot Gris.

"Well, I don't know about it happening to normal people, but it definitely happens to people with a reputation like Chris Dailey." Tom patted her hand in a comforting way. "I don't think you and your family should worry about this too much. You guys weren't even connected to Dailey."

She grimaced. "Well, unfortunately we kind of were connected. I know you heard about Ben being considered a suspect. I mean, he had an argument with the guy the night before he got murdered. And now, this reporter lady I knew from high school is trying to drag the family back into the murder investigation even though Ben has been cleared!" Madeline realized he had raised her voice and saw a few bar patrons turn their heads towards her.

She lowered her voice and continued. "I know our team doesn't have a connection to Dailey, but from what you told me, it sounds like there is a major connection between him and the Barnstable owner. Have you told the police about this?"

"Of course. When they found out he was styling himself as a local scout, they got in touch with a bunch of us to inquire about his life. Not a lot of us had contributed, but I did tell them about the connection that I heard about with William Chase." Tom checked his watch and motioned to the bartender for the check. "I have to get going. There is this kid I need to check out at the college in Milton. Hopefully we can do this again, but next time without all the murder."

He winked at her and put a twenty down to pay the bill. She offered to pay her share, but he waved her off. So that was nice. She got a free dinner and free drinks. She could get used to that. Checking the time, she found it was only seven o'clock. The Red Sox game was just coming on and she sent a quick text to Davis to see if he wanted to discuss what she had found out. After she waited a few minutes with no response, she finished off her drink and made her way to the parking lot.

As she unlocked her car, she decided to just reconnect with him the next day. She made the short drive back to her house thinking about everything Tom had told her. She wondered if the police thought William Chase was a serious suspect. And why was Jennifer so set on blaming her family? All questions she decided could wait until the morning. Putting the game on in the living room, she contented herself to snuggle with the cats and catch the Red Sox in hopefully another win.

Chapter Fifteen

The next morning, she woke up at her usual time for a workday. Her internal clock always woke her up before the sunrise. Of course, her cats also contributed to the early wake up calls. They were never content to let her sleep in. The only difference that day was that she didn't have to be in the office until after lunch. Since there were no camps over the weekend, and the game wasn't until later, she could take the morning off before spending the rest of the day at the park.

Her three cats looked at her while she puttered around the living room picking things up. The cats weren't used to seeing her in the middle of the day, and she felt like she was cutting into their all-important nap time. Her family liked to tease her about her three cats, but she felt a sense of responsibility after rescuing them and giving them a good home. If it made her a crazy cat lady, so be it. Remy, Dewey, and Pedey were named after some of her favorite Red Sox players ever. Her grandfather had a soft spot for those guys, and she grew up with a soft spot for them, too.

After a shower and quick breakfast, she turned on the TV to catch the end of the morning news before flipping over to ESPN to catch the baseball highlights. Groaning, she caught the image of Jennifer Roberts standing in front of the Abington Armadillos ballpark holding a microphone and staring into the camera.

"And now we go live to Jennifer Roberts standing outside the Abington ballpark with more information."

"Thank you, Steve. I'm standing here out front of the ballpark where just three weeks ago, a man was murdered in the visitor's dugout in a vicious manner. Christopher Dailey, a local scout affiliated with the Barnstable Barnstormers was found beaten to death with a baseball bat after being seen arguing with the son of the Boucher family, owners of the Abington team. While the police haven't made any arrests, through diligent investigative work I have found several members of the Abington team were known associates of Mr. Dailey and might have been part of a crime ring involving steroids with the victim. As always, I will keep ahead of this story and bring you news as it breaks. Jennifer Roberts, Channel 5 news, back to you, Steve."

Madeline threw the remote at the TV, missing it by an inch. That woman was infuriating! What kind of information was she getting and from whom? This was the first time Madeline had heard about any of the Abington players being on the wrong side of the law, and the police sure as heck hadn't said anything yet.

She remembered talking to the team manager a few days ago and he was adamant that his guys were clean. Was that just about the steroids? Or were they possible secret gamblers instead?

Pacing round her living room, she clenched and unclenched her fists. She slowed her breathing, trying to calm down, and picked up the phone to call her parents to see if they saw the news report. She noticed two texts from Davis and one from Tom flashing on her screen. She was so engrossed in the story that she missed hearing the buzz alert of the messages.

The text from Tom said he had some more information about William Chase that she'd probably be interested in. The two texts from Davis were checking in on how the conversation with Tom went the night before and one checking to see if she had seen the news this morning.

Madeline sent a quick message back to Tom asking if he wanted to meet for coffee before work. She was intrigued as to what kind of information he could've gotten in one night. Then, she sent a quick message to Davis where she told him she would talk about everything when she got into the office that afternoon. The information would keep for a few more hours. Especially if she could get more information from Tom when they went to coffee.

Tom responded that he would meet her at the Dunkin' Donuts closest to the stadium later that morning. She still had time to check in with her mom to see if she heard about the accusations Jennifer Roberts was throwing around that morning. She had a little over an hour before she would be meeting Tom.

She let the phone ring for a few minutes and then left a message asking her mom to call her back when she got a chance. She was probably busy getting ready for the next games, so maybe she didn't see the report yet. Madeline just wanted to keep her parents away from all the drama if at all possible. The last thing they needed was more stress around game days.

Madeline grabbed her purse and left with a quick goodbye to the cats. She knew that it was crazy to talk to her pets, but those cats seemed to like her talking to them. "Okay guys, I'm heading out. Wish me luck!"

She locked the door behind her and looked around the neighborhood. Shivering, even though it wasn't cold, she could swear that someone was watching her. The neighborhood seemed empty. There weren't any strange cars on the street, and since she lived on a dead end, she knew most of the people in the neighborhood. Even though it was quiet, she still had a weird, eerie feeling.

She tried to put the uneasy feeling out of her mind. The sun was shining, it was a beautiful day, and she had a coffee meeting with a cute guy. Granted, the meeting was about murder and death, but she was still getting out of the house, so it was a win.

The traffic was light on the South Shore after the morning commute, most people leave early to beat traffic to Boston. People tried to avoid the crushing congestion of the standard rush hour. That was something Madeline definitely didn't miss. Her commute was so much better now, that if she was a better person, she would probably bike to work. Of course, she had a somewhat unhealthy aversion to working out, so she was not about to start doing that. Her workouts consisted of walking the ballpark and that was pretty much it.

Madeline pulled into the Dunkin' Donuts parking lot about ten minutes before she was supposed to meet Tom. She took the chance to get her usual drink of a medium iced tea with two sugars. She looked at the selection of donuts, she knew she wasn't going to miss out on getting one. She chose a Boston Crème donut dripping with chocolate frosting. She hoped she could wolf it down before Tom showed up.

She had just finished the donut when Tom walked in the front door. Dressed casually in khakis and a Red Sox polo shirt, he looked like he just stepped out of a baseball program. He stepped up to the counter and ordered a black coffee before joining Madeline at her table.

She must have looked eager because he broke into a smile right away. "So, I guess you want to know what I found out about William Chase last night? Or would you rather talk about the bullpen meltdown during the Sox game last night?"

"C'mon man! Don't leave me hanging! Of course, I want to hear what you know. There is just something about that guy I really don't like." Madeline almost jumped out of her chair in excitement.

"Well, this is a good piece of gossip that I got from my mother actually. She apparently knew William's family from years ago. Since his parents died several years ago, she's lost touch with the family. She was pretty close with his mother, and from her she learned that he had a great uncle that was part of Whitey Bulger's crew in South Boston."

She gasped. "NO!"

"Yup, apparently he was tangentially involved with some of the shenanigans with that group. Now, it didn't seem like the uncle and little William were all that close, but they did see each other at family functions in Southie." Tom leaned closer over the table. "But now it turns out that William had idolized his uncle for a long time. In his office there is a large picture of said uncle with the former owners of the Red Sox. I don't know if that means anything, but it definitely seemed like another piece of the puzzle you might want to know about."

Everyone in the greater Boston area knew about Whitey Bulger and his criminal gang from the late 70s and 80s. He grew up in South Boston and became one of the well-known crime bosses of the era. He was rumored to have been involved as an informant of the FBI, but still perpetuated several murders without the law catching on. There were also links to him and the Isabella Steward Gardner heist, one of the most intriguing crimes of the decade. Several paintings were cut from their frames in the well-known museum and have disappeared. Before Whitey could go on trial, he fled and was on the run with his Southie girlfriend. It still boggled the mind that it had taken the cops over 25 years to find him.

It was big news in Massachusetts when he was finally captured in California, and even bigger news when he was actually convicted and sent to prison. Even more shocking was when he was found dead in prison only a few years after the conviction. It was a big deal. In her previous corporate life, she had several co-workers from South Boston who all had their own stories about Whitey and his crew. Who knows if the stories were true or not, but it made the workdays more interesting.

Madeline leaned back her chair and took a big sip of her drink. Tom looked at her with a smile on his face. He knew that it was good information. She thought about all he told her for a minute. "Wow, that's crazy. And wasn't Chris Dailey a Southie kid too? I wonder if they knew each other better than everyone thought. Make sure to thank your mom for this information."

Tom laughed. "She was definitely excited to dish some gossip. When I told her that you were looking into the murder at the ballpark, she couldn't wait to get and give the scoop."

She laughed along with Tom. Nothing like gossipy ladies to help solve a crime. As she laughed, she made a realization. She had never asked him about that fight she overheard with the player's father. What was his name, Rich? She didn't want him to think that she was stalking him or anything, but she definitely wanted to find out what the deal was. Before she could ask him, he stood up.

"Hey, this was great, but I have to get going. I have some stuff to do at the club before coming out for the game tonight. I have my eye on the pitcher from the other team. He might be looking to break into the affiliated leagues after today. Next time we do this, we'll get dinner." He gave her a quick smile, a wave, and then was out the door.

Well, next time she was for sure going to bring up the argument she overheard. Just because he was cute didn't mean he could get a free pass. She remembered hearing the father mention something about murder but found it hard to believe that Tom would keep good information from her and the police. She assumed the police didn't know anything about it, otherwise they would've questioned Tom and she for sure would've heard about that. She remembered that she planned to meet Davis at the ballpark around this time and resolved to ask him if he knew anything about Tom and Rich. She felt she had so much to tell him and didn't even know where to start.

The game wasn't scheduled until seven that night, under the lights, so the late morning and afternoons were to finalize any promotional items, work with the people performing the Anthem, and answer questions on social media. The team tried to keep fans in the loop as much as possible so they felt invested in the team and continued to follow the Armadillos.

Madeline threw her purse onto her desk, turned on her computer, and walked down towards Davis' office while it warmed up.

Davis was there behind his desk, tapping away on his laptop. His office had several monitors set up to view security cameras. His responsibilities didn't include monitoring the cameras, but he liked to keep an eye on things anyway. The main security office was located closer to the clubhouse where the players went in and out, and there was even a drunk tank in case any fans got too rowdy during games. Luckily, the team didn't have to use it much. Not a ton of people got drunk at the minor league games; it tended to be a more family affair.

Davis looked up at Madeline's knock on the door. "Hey, Maddie, how was your morning?"

"Well, I'm glad you asked. But first, any update on the investigation from the police? Are they any closer to finding out who the killer was?"

"The police don't actually report to me, Maddie. I only get updates from Detective Stephenson periodically. He hasn't contacted me recently though. From what I hear, they are closing in on a suspect and there might be an arrest soon. I don't know who it is or when it's going to happen. So far it's just a rumor."

Madeline nodded and took the seat across from him. "Well, hopefully that'll calm some of this craziness down. I can't keep turning on the TV and seeing Jennifer reporting that someone involved with the team is a murderer. Speaking of which, I did get some interesting facts from Tom last night and this morning about Christopher Daily and his life."

Davis leaned forward in his chair and whistled. "This morning, too? Must've been a good date."

Madeline waved a hand. "No. No. Not like that. We met for coffee this morning because he found out some interesting tidbits of Dailey's life that he thought I'd find interesting. Like the fact that apparently William and Chris might have known each other through Southie connections. William Chase's uncle was involved in the whole Whitey Bulger thing, and Chris Dailey just happened to grow up in the same neighborhood! So, they definitely know each other. Isn't that the type of connection we were looking for? Maybe that's what William wants to meet with me about."

"You know, you might be on to something. He has been around an awful lot. And seems to want to meet with you specifically and not your parents, so it must be something more personal than team business. I'm not sure what that might mean, but hopefully the police will clear this situation for good sooner rather than later. Any other news you need to tell me?" Davis leaned back and put his arms around his chest.

"Nope, that was all the info I got from Tom. I'm going to take a quick walk around the park to see if everything is pretty much in order for tonight's game. Yell if you need anything." Madeline hopped up out of the seat and waved as she made her way out the door back to her office.

She did a quick check of her email. Not seeing anything too important, she decided everything could hold for another half hour. She stashed her purse under her desk, grabbed her cell phone and radio and walked to the home plate section of the park. That was the best time of day. No fans, just a few team members and grounds crew working on the infield. It was peaceful. The team had a shortened practice, so by the time she walked the perimeter of the park, they were heading back to the clubhouse. She gave Billy a quick wave and made her way back into the office.

As she approached the front office area, she saw Detective Stephenson leading her brother out of the office door. Davis was with them looking grim. Her parents were standing by the front desk, her mom crying into her dad's shoulder.

She looked back to Ben who was on his way out the door and noticed his hands behind his back.

"This can't be happening!" She exclaimed to the group. They all looked over at her as she stood in the front door.

"Madeline, we found evidence that your brother was responsible for the murder of Christopher Dailey. He is currently under arrest and we are taking him down to the station. If you don't mind, could you please move?" Detective Stephenson gestured to the doorway behind Madeline.

As she stood there paralyzed by the tableau in front of her, Davis grabbed her arm and pulled her into a hug. As she burrowed her head into his shoulder, the police guided Ben out of the door and to the front entrance of the ballpark. Her father ran into his office and picked up the phone. She assumed he was calling the family lawyer, and her mom grabbed her keys from her office. They looked over at her and Davis.

"We're going down to the station. Madeline, can you please hold down the fort here with Davis just in case anything else goes wrong? One of us will be back by the time the game starts tonight. And no media!" Her mother nodded, content that Madeline and Davis could handle things, and made her way out the door.

Madeline nodded at her mother's retreating back. Of course, she wouldn't talk to the media. This was all their fault anyway. There was no way her brother murdered that guy. Jennifer Roberts just kept stirring the pot and made the police turn their attention back to her family. Davis guided her over to her office and shut the door behind them.

"Madeline. Are you okay?"

"Of course I'm not okay!" She exploded and threw her hands in the air. She turned towards the window that overlooked the parking lot. She watched the police cruiser drive away with her brother in the backseat. Not ten seconds later her parents SUV tore out of the parking lot to follow the police to the Abington station. "My brother has been arrested for a murder that happened at my ballpark to some guy who no one even liked or even knows! I mean, what kind of evidence do the police have? That he fought with the guy? It sounds like a lot of people did that. Plus, I thought he had an alibi. Davis, what do you know about this arrest?" She turned her attention back to him.

"Well," Davis began uncomfortably, squirming in his seat. "They just said they got an anonymous tip that a connection between Chris and your brother would be found in his office. They didn't say what it was, but since your brother did fight with the victim before his murder, they found that to be probable cause to search his office." He wiped a hand over his face. "They found a vial that contained the same type of steroids that Dailey was selling to other teams. That, and his alibi apparently can't be confirmed."

"What! That's crazy! He would never help someone deal steroids. I still bet that Jennifer Roberts has something to do with this. Let me guess, she's camped out in front right now, probably got some great roll of my brother being carted off to jail. Why does she want to ruin my family so much?" Madeline paced across the floor of her small office. Hearing a dinging noise, she looked down at her phone and saw several text messages from her friends trying to find out what was going on.

Eliza came running into the office, knocking quickly on the door. Not waiting for an answer she just came in and shut the door right behind her. "Maddie, it's crazy out there. You won't believe what's happening. There are reporters banging on the front office doors trying to get a comment. I'm not sure how they got in the front gates, but I didn't know where I could hide. I remember you and Davis were back here in the office. Davis, I'm glad you're here, is there any way your guys can get rid of the vultures outside?"

Davis took out his cellphone and dialed his security officer who was in charge of the field level access. "Dan, can you come up here for some crowd control? There seems to be some reporters who got into the ballpark and we need to move them outside the front entrance of the park. From there they can do their reporting, just not inside the ballpark at this time." He waited for a minute. "Thanks, man."

He hung up the phone and looked at the two ladies in front of him. "Guys, we'll move the reporters, but we should probably still issue some sort of statement. Hopefully that will mollify them for a little bit longer. Or at least until an arraignment or another arrest."

"Oh, the police will have another suspect. There is no possible way my brother murdered anyone or was dealing steroids to the team. It's just not the type of guy he is. He loves this team just like the rest of the family and wouldn't jeopardize it for anything!" She realized she was yelling and took a deep breath to try and calm down.

Davis held his hands up as if in surrender. "I get it. I'm just preparing you for any eventuality. I'm going to see if I can get in touch with any police contacts to find out more about this phone call and evidence they found. Maybe it'll turn out to be a big misunderstanding. Now, I'm going to head out to make those calls. Keep me appraised if you get any new information, Maddie."

She nodded as he opened the door and left her office. She sank into her office chair and put her head in her hands. Everything was just happening too fast. She needed time to think.

Eliza peeked out the door and saw that the reporters had all moved away from the front office door. "Man, I was not looking forward to having to deal with all those reporters. Did you know that Jennifer Roberts was one of them out there yelling at me to open up? Does she know who she's talking to? I mean, really." She looked back at Madeline and gave her a sympathetic smile. "Are you going to be okay, sweetie?" She reached over and took one of Madeline's hands.

Madeline sighed. "Not really, Eliza. I mean, I lose my job, come home to the baseball family, and now my brother is arrested for murder. I thought I would have a normal few weeks before things got too dramatic around the ballpark. I guess now my parents are going to depend on me to handle this situation today and I don't even know what to do. Hopefully they'll call with good news from the station soon. I guess I'll be okay, but I'm just going to take a few minutes to process everything. You don't need to stay."

Eliza looked at her for a few seconds, nodded, and then left, shutting the door behind her. Madeline was trying really hard not to cry. She couldn't imagine what her brother must be going through, and her poor parents. No one in the family had ever been in trouble with the law before, so she couldn't even imagine the ringer everyone was going through at the station. All she knew about processing and jail was from reruns of cop shows, and it was not a great place to be hanging out to keep your sanity. She did a quick internet search of the South Shore Sherriff's department to see where they keep people that were arrested before their arraignments.

Not finding any helpful information, she closed her laptop in frustration and turned her chair to face the window. Taking a few deep breaths, she calmed herself down a bit. The family lawyer was a good guy who would do everything he could to help Ben out. She knew what she had to do. She had to find the real killer and clear her brother's name. To do that, she had to talk to William Chase. He seemed to be the key to this whole mess. He knew the victim, had shady dealings with him in the past, and had been awfully anxious to talk to her for the past few weeks. He must have more information.

Before she could hightail it out the door to track down William Chase in Barnstable, she remembered that the press was still waiting outside for some sort of statement. Plus, they had a game in just six more hours. She couldn't believe that it was just after 1 p.m. She thought they should stick with the game schedule, no cancellations, and business as usual. The extent of the statement was going to follow the usual "no comment, see the police for details" until further notice.

Madeline ran out to Eliza's desk, clutching her purse in one hand and her cell phone in the other. She gave Eliza a quick rundown on what to say if anyone called the office looking for scoops and also told her she was going to be out for a few hours to run an errand. Eliza looked at her funny for a few seconds, and then nodded her agreement. After promising to keep her cell phone on, Madeline braced herself to face the horde of reporters outside.

There were about five different people standing out front of the ballpark with various modes of recording equipment. She counted two TV stations, including Jennifer's, and three reporters holding cell phones with what looked like the voice recording app open. She gave Dan, the security guard, a tap on the arm to get by, took a deep breath, and held up her hand to the reporters.

"Okay, guys, I have just a quick statement for you at this time. Basically, the team has no comment regarding the current situation and instead refer you to the Abington Police Department and the South Shore Sherriff's Department if you have any questions." She gave them her sternest look when they began to ask questions as she walked towards her car. All five followed her but backed away as soon as she started the car. No one was looking to get run over for this story. In the mood she was in? She couldn't guarantee that she would press the brakes if they got in front of her car. Not the best thing to do, but it would probably feel pretty satisfying.

She shook her head, and saw Jennifer Roberts standing off to the side fluffing her hair and talking to her cameraman. She made eye contact with her as she pulled out of the parking lot. Jennifer gave a little smiled and wagged her fingers at Madeline. Madeline pressed her mouth together and pulled on to the street next to the park on the way to the highway. Even with all the drama, the day was beautiful. Madeline powered the windows in her blue Honda Accord down and started to blast her Britney Spears mix off her phone through the speakers. She figured by not calling ahead, William would be caught unaware and wouldn't have time to think of a story about how he knew Dailey. She was determined she was going to get to the bottom of everything and he would not get away with it if he was involved.

Chapter Sixteen

The trip to the Barnstable Barnstormers stadium took just under an hour on Route 3 for Madeline. Since it was a beautiful weekend, traffic was pretty steady all the way down to Cape Cod. Surprisingly, there was only a two-mile back up leading to the Sagamore Bridge. The summer months were usually so much worse trying to get on the Cape. She remembered one time there was a ten-mile backup to get over the bridge.

The Boucher family had a beach house on the Cape for as long as she could remember. She had some family that lived out there year-round, too. With baseball season falling right into prime beach season, they usually took advantage of the off-season to hit the beach cottage. It was much less crowded after Labor Day and still warm enough to enjoy the beach until the end of September. Plus, when the season was over the family could relax just that much more.

Crossing over the bridge, she knew she had about ten minutes before she arrived at the Barnstable stadium. Right off the highway, it was centrally located on the Cape for people to get to. Since the Cape Cod Baseball League only ran through July, the Barnstormers were the only other baseball game in town until their season ended after Labor Day weekend. Since there were only five teams in the greater Boston area, including New Hampshire and Rhode Island, the Armadillos played the Barnstable team a lot. One member of the family attended every game, just to keep up-to-date on all the players and other teams. She tried to think of the upcoming baseball schedule. She thought the next game against the Barnstormers was scheduled for about two weeks away.

Madeline pulled into the parking lot of their stadium and found only two other cars parked haphazardly in the front parking spaces. One, a gleaming silver Porsche looked like it pulled in quickly and didn't even make sure their lights were off yet. Even though the sun was out, the lights on the car were on and throwing two bright beams on the front gate of the ballpark. The other, a more sedate black Toyota sedan was parked nearby.

The Barnstable stadium was much newer than the Abington stadium and had a completely different setup. The front offices actually faced the outside of the park and their entry way was outside of the park. The Abington offices were only accessible through the interior of the park.

Madeline put the car in park and tried to come up with a plausible reason to stop by out of the blue. Might as well stick to the truth. She knew William Chase was looking for her the past few weeks, so she'd just tell him she was in the neighborhood and decided to stop by. Hopefully, he hadn't heard about her brother's arrest yet. She wanted to gauge his reaction to the news for herself.

As she walked towards the front door of the offices, she realized how quiet it was out there. She had thought they had a game that night, but the park looked so empty. She checked her watch and saw that it was only 1 p.m., so maybe they just hadn't come in yet. Maybe they set everything up the day before. They had lights, so she assumed that the game was at night. When the Abington team installed lights, night games became hugely popular during the summer.

The front office door was unlocked, so she pushed the door open and slowly walked inside. The front reception desk was empty.

"Hello? Is anyone here?" She called to the empty office. No one responded. She looked behind the front desk, and it looked like whoever sat there just stepped away. The computer was still on, and Madeline noticed a purse underneath the desk. She didn't want to wait, so she walked down the small hallway leading to a couple of offices and large conference rooms.

She had been in these offices a few times, mainly with her father as his assistant before college. She took notes in meetings and generally tried to stay awake. She vaguely knew her way around the small office. She knew that William would have the largest office, probably at the end with all the windows facing the park.

Madeline heard the whir of the air conditioner kick on and shivered. It was always so cold in offices. She even kept a heater, gloves, and a blanket in her own office. Her choice of summer outfit today did not protect against the cold office chill. She wasn't sure if it was just the cold or the eerie quiet in the office that caused her to shiver.

Still not seeing any movement anywhere, she tentatively knocked on William's office door. After no response, she tested the doorknob. It was locked.

"Excuse me." A sharp voice from behind her caused her to jump. "Can I help you with something?"

Madeline turned and faced an older lady, probably in her late fifties with a severe gray bun and glasses, tapping her foot impatiently. She looked at William's door and back to the woman and tried to decide if she should lie. Madeline decided the truth wasn't too bad, so she went with that.

"Hi, there was nobody up front when I got here, and I knew William was anxious to talk to me, so I decided to head back to his office." Madeline pointed at the door with a rueful smile.

"And you might be who?" The woman asked, arching an eyebrow and crossing her arms over her chest.

"Oh, right. I'm Madeline Boucher. My family owns the Abington Armadillos. Do you know if Mr. Chase is around?"

She gestured for Madeline to follow her back to the front of the office. Madeline followed her dutifully, glancing one more time at William's closed office door. As the woman settled behind her desk, she clicked a few buttons on her computer and pulled up what looked like a calendar. Madeline was standing next to her, so she could see everything the woman was looking at. She assumed it was William's calendar. She saw a big red "x" on today's date. That seemed weird. She could've sworn they had a game that night. Why wouldn't he be around on game day?

"It looks like Mr. Chase is out of the office today. Can I set up an appointment for you at a later date?" She peered down at the screen. "How about next week sometime?"

Madeline must have had an annoyed look on her face, because the woman leaned back her in seat and folded her arms. Shutting her computer off, she said "How about you just call when you can make an appointment?"

Madeline nodded and walked towards the front door, still wondering why it was so empty at the ballpark. As she rested her hands on the door frame, she turned back towards the receptionist. "Is there a game scheduled tonight? I could've sworn you guys were playing Lynn tonight. Is that still happening?"

Obviously not too happy to continue to talk to Madeline, the woman huffed. "Yes, the game was rescheduled to tomorrow due to field issues that need to be resolved."

"Thanks, I appreciate ALL your help." Madeline walked out with her head held high. She was not going to let this cranky old broad intimidate her. She heard the woman give a snort behind her. To quote her favorite show as a child, "How rude!" Just because she may have caught Madeline attempting to snoop around the office doesn't give her the right to be so mean. Okay, maybe it did. She would want Eliza to be the same if she caught someone skulking around Madeline's office. She thought she had a free pass with an empty office, but that old battle axe of a receptionist caught her red handed.

The game being rescheduled was weird though. The glimpse at his calendar showed a whole day blocked off. She wondered if that was significant. She was going to have Eliza check with the Lynn team to see if they had other information about why the game changed.

Back in her car, she turned her phone radio to the "boy band" station. Sometimes a person just needed some good old pop tunes to make the drive go quicker. Making sure the Bluetooth was connected, she cranked the music through the car speakers.

Well, she couldn't worry about not getting information from William today. She had to regroup back at the office and figure out next steps. She hoped that by the time she was back at the office, there would be an update on her brother. She still couldn't believe the police arrested him. She needed to find out if Davis got any more information out of the detectives. Since the rest of the family was caught up in that mess, it was up to her to make sure the day's game went off without a hitch.

The team was playing the Weymouth Windjammers that night, and she needed to make sure all the pre-game events were set-up and everyone knew where to be. They had another local group singing the National Anthem and then a local business guy was throwing out the first pitch. He donated a lot of money to some local charities, and they wanted to recognize all he'd done. Madeline was now in charge of making sure the gentleman knew exactly what he was supposed to do. Usually her mother coordinated the first pitch ceremonies, but Madeline knew she was going to be a bit preoccupied at the moment.

The drive didn't take nearly as long as before since she was flying against traffic to the Abington ballpark. As she pulled into the parking lot, she noticed the same five reporters hanging out smoking cigarettes and leaning against their cars. At the sound of her car pulling in they all jumped up and tossed their cigs into the parking lot. Grimacing in frustration, Madeline tried to park as close to the entrance as she could in hopes of trying to avoid them.

Unfortunately, she wasn't so lucky. She heard one shrill voice out of the group of reporters that made her turn her head. Running up from behind the group of five was Jennifer Roberts with her microphone outstretched and her cameraman in tow. Madeline felt her face get hot and took a deep breath.

"Madeline Boucher, do you have any comment about your brother, the murderer?" Shoving her microphone in Madeline's face, she looked at her with a satisfied smirk on her face. Madeline had a moment of rage where she instantly regretted not being able to punch her full in the face. Taking another deep breath, Madeline looked the camera in the lens, and spoke directly to her viewers.

"The team has no comment other than to say we support Ben Boucher and hope the police will realize they have an innocent man in custody. We are fully cooperating with the authorities and don't put much stock in anonymous reports being perpetuated in the media. A little research would go a long way in learning there is something more involved in this investigation. We support the South Shore Sherriff's office in their quest to bring resolution to this investigation." Madeline looked back at Jennifer who didn't look as smug as she did minutes ago. Madeline thought that Jennifer was probably expecting some sort of blow-up or confrontation to get a good sound bite for her nightly report.

Madeline gave her a fake smile, turned around, and walked quickly through the front gate with Dan, the security guard, barring entrance to the reporters yelling questions. She scurried to the front office and got inside the door without any more trouble. Resting her back against the door, she sighed at Eliza and said, "Thank goodness that's over for today."

Eliza looked up from her computer and muted her headset. "How'd it go at the Barnstable stadium?"

"Not great." Madeline shrugged and rested her elbows on the top of Eliza's desk. "He wasn't even there. The park was completely empty. I did meet the, um, authoritative lady at the front desk though. She caught me trying to get into William's office."

Eliza laughed. "Oh no! What did you think you were going to find? Plus, I should've warned you about that lady. Her name is Edith. She's been part of that office for as long as I can remember. Well before William bought the team. She's probably a Cape institution at this point. I bet he's afraid to fire her."

"Good to know. Well, at least I found out that the game they were supposed to play tonight got rescheduled. She didn't give me a very good reason though. Something to do with the field, but it sounds like a lie to me. Could you maybe put in a call to the receptionist over at the Lynn team to find out what reason they were given for the change? I didn't want to push my luck with Edith. She couldn't wait to get me out of there."

Eliza looked through her rolodex of numbers on her desk. "Sure, I've got the number for the Lynn Ramblers right here. Give me a few minutes to see what I can learn and then I'll come find you."

Thanking her for helping out, Madeline went to her office and shut the door behind her. She pulled out her laptop and logged into the team email system. Waiting there was an email from the gentleman who was supposed to throw out the first pitch that night. He was canceling due to the arrest of her brother. He didn't want his name or charity work associated with a potential murderer.

Madeline sighed dramatically and put her head in her hands. With such short notice, she didn't think she'd be able to pull anyone for the first pitch ceremony. She decided the team would forgo it for that night. The local singers sent an email that said they were still committed to sing. They had known the family for years and wouldn't let the investigation keep them from supporting the family and team. There were several other emails from various outraged members of the local community about her brother being a bad role model to their children. What ever happened to "innocent until proven guilty?" There were also emails from avid season ticket holders and baseball fans pledging their support for the team and the family.

She closed down her emails and looked at the messages left on her desk by Eliza while she was gone. She couldn't get Eliza to just transfer people to her voicemail. Eliza liked doing things the old-fashioned way. Nothing seemed too urgent; mostly just requests or interviews from the media. Madeline placed a quick call down to Billy in the manager's office to let him know that the players should probably refrain from speaking to the media about the situation. They didn't want any issues or misunderstandings with the players. Billy readily agreed and said he would hold a team meeting before the game to let them know. Madeline let him know that she would stop down to give the family line about the investigation, so the players would understand that they were all in this together.

Madeline heard her phone make a quick pinging noise to let her know she received a text. Looking down, she saw it was from her mom. They got her brother released and they were taking him back to the house to lay low for a while. She let her know that they'd be back in the office the next day, but to call her if there were any problems.

Madeline waited approximately ten minutes before picking up the phone to get the details from her mother. She wanted to make sure she waited long enough to let them get settled at home first. She didn't want to bother them if they were still at the station.

After about five rings, her mom picked up, "Hello?"

"Hey, Mom, it's me."

"Yes, I know. I do have caller ID." She said with a tired tone. "Sorry, Madeline, to be so short with you, it's just things are a bit sideways at the moment."

Madeline sighed and tried to keep from crying at the sound of her mom's voice. "Yeah, things are weird now. How are you guys holding up? What did the lawyer have to say? Why did Ben's alibi fall through? They don't really think he killed Dailey, do they?"

Her Mother took a deep breath. "Calm down, Maddie. I'm fine. Your brother is fine. Your father is fine. We're just wrung out from the police station. The lawyer said the police didn't really have any good evidence, so after questioning him they released him and told him not to leave town. That's why we brought him back to the house. He's going to lay low here for a little while."

Madeline heard her "shush" someone in the background. She assumed it was her father trying to interrupt. Her parents had a system when it came to talking to their kids on the phone. One usually started the conversation and the other would attempt to butt in as many times as they could. They forget that a person could talk as long as they wanted to on the phone now.

"Look, Maddie, your father and I are going to be coming in first thing in the morning to get ready for the next game. Is there anything serious happening for tonight's game that we need to worry about?"

Madeline looked down at the media messages and the cancellation email from the first pitch guy. She decided it was stuff that could wait until she saw them the next day. "No, Mom, don't worry about it. Just make sure you guys take care of each other and I'll talk to you either later tonight or tomorrow."

Hanging up the phone, Madeline swiveled around in her chair to face the window. Everything was just weird. She forgot to get the answer about Ben's alibi. She thought that cleared him weeks ago. She wondered what changed since he was cleared. And the police found evidence in his desk? Who called in the anonymous tip? What was the deal with William Chase?

Unfortunately, she had more questions than answers at that point, and she had to keep the baseball team going until everything was cleared up. No problem. She'd only been there for a month and now seemed to be in charge of baseball operations when her family was out of commission. Awesome.

Checking her watch, she realized the team practice was probably almost over and they'd be having their team meeting soon. She grabbed her phone and headed down to the home field clubhouse. Waiting in the front video room was Billy and the team. She gave them a quick smile and then launched into the family statement including what their next steps were. Luckily the team had been with them for a long time, and none of the players seemed all that concerned about events. After the meeting, several players came up to her to offer their thoughts and to help if they could.

This team was a family and she wouldn't have it any other way.

Chapter Seventeen

The time before the game went by in a blur of emails, phone calls, and meetings with vendors in the park. The family wanted to reassure everyone that the team was fully cooperating with the police and that the investigation was ongoing. After speaking with some advertisers and corporate sponsors, Madeline felt that everyone was still all in with the Abington Armadillos and were just waiting for this investigation to be resolved so they could get on with the season.

Eliza gave her a quick wave as she left the ballpark before the game. She wasn't required to stay for the late games, knowing she had a family to get home to. The game itself went off without a hitch, and the arrest of her brother didn't seem to dry up attendance. Madeline breathed a sigh of relief knowing that she didn't screw things up working by herself.

The game ended with a win for the Abington team, and Madeline waited until everyone had exited the park to lock up. There were a few people still milling about, mostly the security team, so Madeline didn't feel anxious about being by herself. She realized she hadn't seen Davis since earlier that day; he must have been checking all the security at the park during the game. Ever since the murder, the team had doubled their security checks to make people feel better and to also prevent another incident if possible.

Since it was a summer night, even in the dark the temperature was still warm. The lights of the parking lot made her feel safe as she said goodbye to some of the other workers. As she made her way to the car, she noticed a piece of paper flapping in the night breeze underneath her windshield. Before she could reach out and pluck it from where it rested, she heard her name called out from across the parking lot. Nervous that it was one of the reporters who had been hanging out all day, she steeled herself for another confrontation and turned around.

Heaving a sigh of relief, she saw it was Davis running towards her. She gave him a wave. The reporters must have found someone else to bother, because they weren't anywhere in the parking lot. The only hint of media activity was a news van parked in the back of the lot. There didn't look to be anyone with the van, or in the van either. She was going to have the security team check it out. It seemed very peculiar.

Davis reached her a few seconds later. "Hey, Maddie, things went well tonight, right? I double checked everything with the security team and it looks like everything went well. Great job holding everything together today. I know it's late today, but since there is no game tomorrow night, would you want to go get a bite to eat after work?"

"Thanks for the offer, Davis, but I made a promise to myself that I would head over to my parent's house to see how Ben was holding up. I think we're going to do pizza and beer if you want to join us. I know the family trusts you with all this stuff going on. Plus, you're practically family yourself."

He nodded and glanced over at her front windshield. "Sure, I'll swing by. Hey, what's that paper on your window?" He grabbed the paper before she could check it out.

It was another note written in black marker in block letters.

STOP THE QUESTIONS. YOUR BROTHER IS A MURDERER.

Davis put the note down on the hood of the car and pulled out his cell phone. "I'm calling Detective Stephenson right now; this is another threat directed at you." He waited a moment while the phone rang on the other end. "Hey, Detective, this is Davis from the Abington Armadillos. I know it's late, but I'm outside the ballpark in the lot right now with Madeline Boucher and she just received another note. This time it was placed under the windshield wipers of her car. I'm the only other person who touched the note, and I put it right back down on the hood." He listened for a minute. "Okay, we'll be here. Thanks."

He turned back towards Madeline who was clenching and unclenching her fists. He took her by the shoulders and looked her in the eyes. "Detective Stephenson is on his way. He's still not one hundred percent sure that your brother is actually the killer. He's going to try and pull some prints from the note and from your windshield in hopes we can figure out who is harassing you."

Madeline stood still for a minute, still in shock about being threatened again. Another note? She didn't feel any closer to finding out who the real murderer was, but someone must think she knows more than she does. She wished she did. That would clear her brother's name and erase the dark cloud over the family team.

Not more than five minutes later, the detective's unmarked Toyota sedan pulled into the lot next to her car. Stepping out of the car, he still looked like a character from a movie. No trench coat this time, but he was wearing a fedora tilted jauntily across his head. He took a pair of latex gloves and an evidence bag from his front seat and placed the note inside. Sealing the bag, he turned back to Davis and Madeline.

"Okay guys, I'll take this back to the station to test for any prints. Do you by chance have any security cameras in the parking lot? Maybe we'll get lucky and catch the guy on video."

Davis led Madeline and the detective back through the front entrance. "Sure, follow me. Do we know the time frame we want to look at?" He looked at Madeline for confirmation.

"Well, I got back to my office around one after running some errands. I had to run through a group of reporters standing at the front entrance. I'm not sure what time they left. I had some meetings with the team and then the game. I just left the office about five minutes ago."

The trio wove their way through the park to the main security office. Located right outside the clubhouse entrance, all the cameras were monitored 24 hours a day by a security team run by Davis. He tapped a young guy on the shoulder and asked to see the playback from the time frame discussed. The tapes weren't actual video tapes anymore, instead they were downloaded feeds sent to the cloud server that were purged every few weeks unless needed. Unfortunately for the group, they only showed the parking lot and main entrances to the park and clubhouse. It didn't help in the murder investigation or the break-in, but it did help in the case of the mysterious note.

The three people stepped to the side of the office where a laptop was up and running. Pulling up a seat, Davis sat down and began to click around. Detective Stephenson leaned over the small screen to watch a feed of the parking lot from the afternoon. Madeline tried to stand on her toes to peek over their shoulders, but the screen was too small and she was too short. The two men huddled together and were murmuring quietly to each other when all of a sudden, Detective Stephenson yelled, "There!"

Madeline leaned over the top of Davis' head as the Detective leaned back to let her look. They had paused the picture right as someone was placing the note under her wiper blade. Advancing it slowly, the person turned around until they finally got a look at the front of the person. Unfortunately, the person had a black hooded sweatshirt pulled up over their face, with dark sunglasses obscuring what they might look like. She couldn't even tell if it was a man or woman underneath the dark clothes. She wondered if it was the same person who had broken into her brother's office. She thought they looked about the same height, but the grainy footage didn't provide any clearer details. Looking at the time stamp, she saw that it had to happen about halfway through the game, so the parking lot was quiet.

Madeline turned away from the screen dejectedly, but the men stayed looking a little bit longer. She assumed they were looking to see if the person went somewhere else after leaving her that note. She heard the mouse click a few more times before they called her back to the laptop. They pointed at a car parked near where the news van was parked. The van was still there, and a silver Mini Cooper pulled up next to it. The person who left the note got into the passenger side of the car and it took off. The license plate was unreadable, but she didn't think there would be that many silver Mini Coopers tooling around the South Shore.

The detective used his phone to take pictures of both the person and the car before standing up to his full height. "Madeline, I don't think I have to remind you again to be careful. I'll run this through the police system, see if we get any pings, but for now, just lay low. Your brother has the right idea. Just make sure you stay off the radar of whoever this person is."

Madeline nodded at him, even though now she had more questions.

Chapter Eighteen

The next day, after a supremely uneventful day, Madeline headed to her parents' house to see how her brother was holding up. Ben was in the upstairs guest bedroom that had been outfitted just for him. There was a big screen TV, a streaming video player, and Wi-Fi access so he wouldn't be too out of touch with the real world during his sequestration. She walked in as he was sitting in front of the TV watching the NESN Red Sox wrap-up from the day before. He saw her, put the TV on mute, and waved her in.

"Hey, sis, how goes it at the park?"

She looked at him with concern. "It's fine. The team is fine. How are you holding up, though? I mean, jail wasn't exactly comfortable was it?" She sat on the edge of the bed.

"Yeah, it wasn't the greatest, but I think the police know they got the wrong guy. I'm confident I won't spend any more time there. I mean, other than the one fight I had with him I didn't know Chris from a hole in the wall. That Detective Stephenson guy mentioned they were still investigating and might have more information due to the steroid angle. So for now, to distract myself, I'm going to hole up here and catch up on some reading." He waved a hand to the pile of sports magazines next to the bed.

She rolled her eyes at him and threw a pillow at his head. "Okay, but why did they say your alibi didn't check out? What exactly was your alibi?"

Ben looked down at his hands, and for a minute, she didn't think he was going to answer. Then he sighed and looked back at her. "I didn't want to tell anyone. It was nothing really. I went out the night before and brought someone home with me." Ben's cheeks turned pink, obviously embarrassed to be talking about this with his sister. "But that's not the worst part. I had an interview the next day, the day of the murder."

"An interview!" She said, jumping to her feet. "For what? Are you leaving the Armadillos?"

"No! That's not what this was like at all." He paused. "Okay, maybe it was about that a little bit. It was an interview with the big leagues. With the Red Sox! Can you imagine? Well, I didn't want Mom and Dad to find out until I got more information or got the job. And so, I told the detectives only about the woman I brought home. She, of course, mentioned that I had left early that morning and she wasn't sure why. I'll admit, it wasn't the best idea I'd ever had to not let the police know about the interview."

Madeline shook her head incredulously at her brother. This was too much. So, her party animal brother was more ashamed of having a job interview than bringing a stranger home for the night. Nice. "So, did you finally fess up? I mean, a job interview is infinitely better than being considered for a murder."

He nodded. "Yeah, Mom and Dad know now. They weren't pleased, but it looks like the job might not happen anyway with all this press coverage of how I might be a murderer. Of course, I was on my way to Fenway when the murder allegedly happened, but you know how the internet is. They'll latch on to any whiff of scandal. And I'm sure the Red Sox don't want to be associated with that."

She couldn't believe it. Her brother was interviewing with other people? He was bringing strange women home? The internet was trolling him? What next?

As Madeline tried to decide what to say, her mother called from downstairs. "Time to eat!"

Ben and Madeline trudged down the stairs. What was it about being in a person's childhood home that made one revert back to their youth? She felt like she was sixteen again, getting in trouble and skulking around the house. At least now all the truth was out there. Hopefully, the family would be able to get past this sooner rather than later. Of course, the police finding the actual murderer would make that easier too.

Davis had arrived while Ben and Madeline were still upstairs. He looked as if he just stepped out of a catalog. He must have cleaned up since they last saw each other at the park. Her parents were fawning over him. They loved having him as security lead and friend to the family. She wondered if he visited them more than she even knew about. He seemed so familiar with the house and where to go for dinner. As a group they decided to sit outside on the patio for an outdoor dinner.

"Maddie, bring out the condiments tray, we're having hamburgers and hot dogs. I put everything together, I just don't have enough hands for everything!" Her mom grabbed a tray of burgers and delivered them to her husband and Davis who were manning the grill.

"Okay, now that we're all together, we really need to get to the bottom of all this hoopla. Ben obviously didn't do it, so now the questions remain: who did it and who is leaving threats to Madeline. Those are the big questions, and they must be related, right?" Her mother lit some candles on the outside table and sat down while providing her running commentary about the murder. "I mean, the only way it makes sense is for it to be all connected somehow."

Davis joined the group sitting at the table. "I have to agree." He pointed at Madeline. "You somehow got involved in this mess, Maddie, and now someone thinks you know more about the murder than the police do. That's why you're getting threats."

Madeline looked at him sharply. She didn't tell her parents all the threats she had received recently. Just the one note on her car after the game. She thought back to the person in Ben's office. She was hoping they weren't connected, but it seemed awfully fishy that her brother was the main suspect and she was being threatened. She didn't want her parents to worry unnecessarily. She had things under control with Davis.

"From what I gather, there were a bunch of people who didn't like Chris. Ben is just one of the many that fought with him in the past few months, and we know that David Murphy's dad had problems with him in the past as well. And we can't forget about all the shady crap William Chase has been involved with. I mean, he's been following me around, trying to talk to me about something mysterious. I would bet my paycheck that he's up to his eyeballs in this situation." Madeline took a moment to bite into her steaming cheeseburger. Sighing in contentment, she leaned back in her seat.

"But for real though, I don't know anything! At least nothing I didn't know a few weeks ago. Everything I know I've told Detective Stephenson and Davis. Obviously, it wasn't much because the only thing they did was arrest Ben." Madeline let out a frustrated sigh. "I mean, I'm not the one advancing the story. It's the stupid reporter from high school. Jennifer Roberts has been camped out at the ballpark for days now trying to imply that our team had something to do with Chris Dailey's death."

"Jennifer Roberts? The reporter from the local news?" Her dad asked, placing a plate of hot dogs on the table. "I know that name from somewhere."

"Yeah, Dad, the news. We watch it all the time." Ben said.

"No, that's not it. It'll come to me. But for now, let's eat this food before it gets cold. I see Madeline already dug in." He smiled over at her as she swept a napkin across her face.

The family dug in, and Madeline grabbed a grilled hot dog from the pile. Yes, she had a burger, but there was something about homemade grilled hot dogs that called to her. It might be mystery meat, but fresh off the grill they were delicious in the standard New England split top roll. The meal was rounded out by homemade potato salad, baked beans, and boring salad. Even though she knew she should probably watch her weight, Madeline couldn't resist the picnic food. She resolved to eat more salad starting the next day. Maybe.

The conversation moved from the murder to how the season was progressing. Only a month in and the team seemed destined for the playoffs for the second straight year. The young guys were fitting in well, and the veterans were providing steady guidance to make the team successful. Plus, Billy, the manager, was an old pro who knew how to guide the team to the winner's circle.

Before too long, they noticed the night had crept in and it was getting late. There wasn't a game scheduled for the next day, but it was understood that it was all hands on deck until the murder stuff was solved. She gave her family some hugs and she let Ben know that she would take care of things while he was in seclusion. Luckily, he had kept a bunch of notes about what he did day-to-day to help while she filled in.

Davis walked her out to the car and held the door open for her. "Maddie, any update about the break-in to your brother's office the night of the gala?"

She looked at him. "No, no one is telling me anything. Why? Did you hear something? I mean, I have my suspicions that it was tied together with the note that was left on my car, but the police won't confirm that."

"Well, after talking to Ben and the legal team, I think we can safely assume that the evidence the police found after that anonymous tip was planted. It had to have been planted the night when everyone was out of the office at the gala. Are you sure you don't remember anything about the person who ran into you? And that the video didn't jog any memories?"

Madeline thought back to the night two weeks ago. It seemed much longer than that. She shuddered as she remembered the person running out the back door. "No, I mean, they were about my height, average size I would say. They were wearing all black and the lights weren't on in the office. The video was useless; I couldn't even tell if the person was the same height. I mean, logic would say they were the same, but who knows."

She suddenly straightened. "Wait! I do remember something. The person had gloves on, but I saw some skin peeking out from the end of them. The hand had a thin gold bracelet on it. So that must mean it was a lady, right?" She was excited, leaning over the car door looking at Davis.

"Hold on, Maddie. I don't know, but I'll pass that information onto Detective Stephenson. He may want to talk to you again though, so if you remember anything else, don't forget to tell him or me immediately. He is on our side believe it or not. The arrest of your brother was necessary due to the evidence, but I don't think he believes your brother is guilty. He seems sure the evidence was put there by a third party. Ben being arrested will hopefully cause the real culprit to relax and make a stupid mistake." He went to shut her door. "Be careful and send me a text when you get home. With all those threats you've been getting, I don't want you to take any chances."

Madeline nodded at him through the open car window. As she backed out of her parent's driveway, she gave him a wave. The drive home was filled with thoughts of Davis. He was such a nice guy. It felt good to have someone other than her family care about her well-being. High school Madeline would have never believed that Davis would become so close to her family. She mentally gave her younger self a high five as she pulled into her driveway.

Everything looked the same as it did that morning. It was just about 10 p.m., so there were a few people out walking their dogs for the last time that night. That made her feel a bit safer, seeing other people about. Hopefully, that would deter anyone wishing her harm. So far, she hadn't felt too physically threatened; even when she had surprised the person in the office, she had never felt in danger physically. She just didn't like the unsettledness of it. Someone was following her around, leaving her notes, and even knew where she lived. Hopefully now that the investigation was ramping up again, the person would finally realize she didn't have anything to do with it.

Madeline entered her house and greeted the three cats. She was struck by the absolute silence in the house. After all the craziness of the past few days, it felt nice to come home to a quiet house. She could put her sweatpants on and binge on some old TV. She didn't drink at her parents' house, so she poured herself a little glass of wine and moved into the living room. Pedey snuggled up on her legs while the other two cats staked out positions on the other furniture. Popping the TV on, she flipped channels until she saw Jennifer Roberts' face on the screen. Of course, she was still on the murder beat. Madeline turned the TV up, scaring the cat on her lap. Rubbing the two scratches she now had on her ankle, she turned her attention back to the TV.

"As most of you know, Benjamin Boucher was arrested by police and released for the murder of Christopher Dailey earlier this week. Police are not commenting on the sudden release, but sources say they had found evidence of drug use in Boucher's offices. Those same sources say the Abington team is desperately trying to cover up any connection with the murdered steroid dealer. There are reports that all players and personnel will be tested tomorrow for performance enhancing drugs as a result of this development. At the ballpark, this is Jennifer Roberts, back to you."

Madeline let out an aggravated sound, which was effective in scaring the other two cats from the living room. She jumped off the couch and grabbed her phone. She texted her brother to see if he saw it, and then she texted Davis the same. She wanted to know if there was something they could do to stop the rumors from flying around about the team. Her grandfather always said that they were a team of integrity, and they never would've permitted any type of drugs, performance or otherwise, on the team.

Her brother texted her back, told her to calm down and not worry about it until the next day. Davis also responded to say he didn't see the story. He promised they would talk in the morning at the office but he was sure the rumors were unfounded. She put her phone down, not satisfied. She needed to do something.

Madeline decided to make a list of all the people she suspected of being involved in the whole Chris Dailey fiasco. She thought back to that list that his girlfriend dropped outside the restaurant. The names on that list were familiar to her, all except for one. Brittany Marks. She needed to find out who that person was. It was clearly a list of suspects since her brother's name was on it. The second question was why Ashley had a list of potential murder suspects with her. Did someone give them to her? Was she investigating her boyfriend's murder? Did she even know what the list was?

She pulled the list out of her purse and laid it across her knees.

1.	Ben Boucher
2.	William Chase
3.	Brittany Marks
4.	Walter Lawson
5.	David Murphy
6.	Richard Murphy

She immediately crossed out Ben's name. She knew he wasn't the murderer. David and Richard had a bit too much to lose to commit a crime of that nature in her opinion. That left William Chase, Brittany Marks, and Walter Lawson.

Madeline was making herself crazy with all the questions. Looking at the clock, she saw it hit midnight and she realized how late it really was. Even though there was no game the next day, she wanted to spend most of her time at the ballpark. She needed to get some sleep. Especially because the next day already looked like it was going to be a cluster of epic proportions dealing with the media, easing fans minds, and working with the team to figure out what was going on. That was a lot of balls in the air and she needed to be able to juggle them. She was determined to take as much stress of her parents as possible.

Chapter Nineteen

The alarm on her phone blared at 6:30 a.m. the next morning and she grappled without looking to turn it off. Opening her eyes, she saw the day had dawned bright and clear. A perfect day for the ballpark. She still couldn't keep the anxiety from creeping in; she just had a bad feeling about the day. Shaking off her jitters, she checked her phone before climbing out of the covers.

She wanted to check to see if there were any texts or alerts from after she went to bed the night before. She wasn't expecting any, since she went to bed so late, but it never hurt to check. There was only one text on her phone, and it was from Davis. He just said he had found a connection between the news reports and the Barnstable team. He would tell her more once she got into the office. Now her curiosity was peaked. She took a quick look at the team social media sites, just to make sure nothing crazy was happening there. Madeline knew she had a few hours before everyone would wake up and see the news, and then it would be time for more damage control.

She was glad that Davis had found some sort of connection though. She had no idea what it could be, but it had to be important for Davis to want to tell her about it. Jennifer Roberts seemed to have a personal vendetta against the team and Ben in particular. Madeline wondered why she was adamant that her brother was the murderer when the police had already cleared him and the family of wrongdoing. If she did have some mysterious source, was it a person involved with the team somehow? Did that mean there was a mole in the ballpark? She couldn't see anyone involved with the team spreading rumors and turning on the family.

By the time she got out of her house at eight, the temperature had seemed to soar to a humid eighty degrees. It was going to be a hot one. She didn't mind the heat; it was the humidity that got her. Her short bob hair never looked good when it was humid out. Too poufy. She figured she would go as long as she could before she had to put a hat on for the day to tame her tresses. Hopping into her car, she made it to the park in about ten minutes and parked in front of the gates. There were still a few news vans parked outside, but it didn't seem as hectic as it did the previous few days. She saw her parent's car parked at the far end of the parking lot. They liked the extra exercise in the morning before they started the day. Davis' car was in the lot as well, and she was anxious to get inside and see what he had found out.

The ballpark was still quiet at that point in the morning. On the average non-game day, there wasn't a ton of extra people around. Just the park staff and team. Madeline walked through the front gates with a wave to the security guard at the front. Before heading to her office, she walked through one of the tunnels to the seats. The grounds crew was out on the field watering the infield and pitcher's mound and raking the base paths. It was so peaceful on that day. She knew that things couldn't stay that calm, so she took the moment to breathe in the scent of the ballpark. Ah, freshly cut grass, a hint of wet dirt from the infield, and little bit of leather from the dugouts. After she took another quick meditative breath, she turned to head back to the offices.

Madeline entered the front office, waved at Eliza, and immediately hurried down to Davis' office. He had his head bent over his computer and seemed to be mumbling something to himself as he clicked around his mouse. She rapped the door frame with her knuckles, which caused Davis to snap his head up in surprise.

"Maddie! I'm so glad you're here!" She smiled at his reaction.

"Wow, must be a good piece of gossip you have to tell me. Did you ever see the news story I told you about yesterday?" She asked as she sat down across from him. "That Jennifer Roberts is out there spreading rumors again. Still alleging that we have a steroid issue here at the park. It's getting real frustrating to deal with her and these stories."

"Well, I think I may have found the source of all the rumors. It's not anyone directly related to the team, so we don't have to worry about that. But it is a bit of a sticky issue. The person leaking information is tangentially related to the team." Davis hesitated. "It's David Murphy's father, Richard."

"Richard! David's dad!?" Madeline exclaimed. "But why would he try to sabotage the team like that? David is such an integral part of the Abington Armadillos identity and its success. He seems so happy here." Madeline couldn't believe it.

"I think David is happy here. I found out his father has been shopping him on the market to other teams in the area for a while now. I think he's hoping to get some more money or a better contract for his son. Not that there is a ton of money in the independent league, but David is a hot commodity. He could probably command a decent price on the open market. If the team suffers due to the murder investigation, he might have a way out of his contract." Davis said. "I called your mom earlier to ask about his contract to see if there was anything in it that would give him that idea. She is probably on her way over now to discuss it."

"Did David Murphy know about his father's involvement in the leaks out there?" she asked.

Davis looked back at his computer screen. "It doesn't seem like it. I had the manager call over there today before he came in just to make sure he's still on board with the team 100%. He swore he had no plans to leave the team or that he even wanted to leave the team at all. He promised to talk to his dad about the rumors to find out what went on."

"That must have been what Richard was fighting about with Tom the other day when I overheard them. I told you about that, right?" Davis nodded. "Good, he mentioned something about a deal and that Chris Dailey was involved. I wonder what his part in this whole scheme was. Maybe that's why Chris tried to get friendly with my brother. They were in on the scheme together, Chris and Richard!"

"Settle down, Maddie. I'm still in the gathering information phase right now. Richard Murphy might have been just a guy who thought he was doing the best he could for his son. He might not have had any malicious intent."

"Malicious intent? What do you call impugning the good name of this baseball team and my family in the process? How do we know he wasn't involved in Chris Dailey's murder and is now trying to throw suspicion over on my brother? Hmm? What do you have to say about that?" She crossed her arms and glared at Davis across his desk.

"I don't know, Maddie. But I do know that when he arrives at the park today, I'm going to pull him aside and try to get the real story from him. If he says anything remotely suspicious about Chris Dailey, I'll direct him to the police and they can handle it from there. You can trust me with this, Maddie." Davis held his hands out in supplication.

With a jolt, Madeline realized she trusted Davis wholly. Even though they just recently reconnected, he had done nothing but stand by her side during the whole cluster of a situation. She softened her stance. "Okay, that's fair. But can you call me on the walkie when you take him for a chat? I would like to be there as a representative of the family. Plus, I want to see what he has to say for himself."

"Fine, just don't get too angry until we hear what he has to say." Davis looked down at his watch. "It's still early, but Richard should be arriving with his son any minute now." Picking up the phone, he quickly dialed four numbers which meant he was calling someone in the park. "Billy, could you give me a call when you see Richard Murphy? I want to talk to him about something." He was silent for a moment. "Great, thanks."

Hanging up the phone, he looked back at Madeline.

"We're all set. I'll come get you when Billy calls me back and we'll go calmly talk to Richard Murphy about what he's been up to. Key word is calmly, right?" Davis eyed her with wariness.

"Yes. Fine. Calmly." She said with a roll of her eyes.

Madeline headed back to her office. Plopping down in her desk chair, she swiveled to look outside. Releasing a breath she didn't know she'd been holding, she knew that Davis would help her figure out how to stop the rumors from affecting the rest of the team and the season. If it was just this one guy, they could probably cut off all this drama now. Then the police could actually find the real murderer, instead of all their focus being on Ben.

She resolved to get some work done while she waited to hear from Davis. Her email was pretty full of people inquiring about the team moving forward and if they were planning anything different with all the news coverage. Outside of that one guy canceling his first pitch the other day, most of the emails were supportive. The season ticket holders were really coming through for the team. She answered a few of the emails and sent out "no comment" emails to all the press requests.

Before too long, Davis was tapping on her door and beckoning her to follow him. She assumed that meant that Richard Murphy was in the building and they were going to confront him. She put a hand on her stomach to try and quell the butterflies that were flying around. Confrontation was not her favorite thing, and this was definitely going to be a confrontational subject. Taking a deep break, she stood up and followed Davis down to the team meeting room.

Entering the room, she saw David and his father standing in the back huddled in conversation. Davis walked over, shook both guys' hands and gestured for them to take a seat.

"Richard, I'm sure you've been listening to all the media reports swirling around the team at this time. Recently, I found out that leak was coming from someone related to the organization." Richard looked nervously at his son as Davis spoke. "We traced it back to you. We wanted to come find out the real story and ask that you stop talking to the media without coming to see someone at the front office first." Davis looked at Madeline and she nodded.

David Murphy looked at his dad incredulously. "Dad? Is this true? Have you been spreading the rumors about the steroids?"

Richard Murphy looked down at his shoes and sighed. "Yes, it's true. I thought I was doing what's best for you. I wanted you to get money on the open market. I thought by making the team look bad, other teams would want to get you and Abington would let you go. I just talked to that Jennifer Roberts lady once!" He spread his hands out in a pleading gesture to his son. "I didn't think it would go this far. Chris Dailey gave me the idea a few weeks before he died. He told me this was a good way to get out of David's contract. It just seemed easy."

David looked at his father with widening eyes. He shook his head in disbelief. "Dad, I can't believe this. Why would I want to go somewhere else? Abington has been great to me, and let's be honest; I'm only one or two years away from retirement anyway. Why should I leave here now?"

Richard looked down at his hands again, and then spoke. "Son, it's been a bad couple of years. You don't know this, but my construction business is going through a lean time. I was hoping by getting you a bigger contract, I could stay afloat a little bit longer. I know what I did was wrong and I can't apologize enough." He looked over at Madeline. "Madeline, your family has been great to David and me, and after the first time I talked to Jennifer Roberts, I felt so guilty that I never contacted her again. The first rumor might have been from me, but I haven't talked to her in two weeks. I don't know where the newest report came from, but it wasn't from me."

Madeline looked at him with pity in her eyes. She believed him. He seemed like a good guy in a desperate situation. She knew money problems sometimes made people do crazy things. "Richard, I believe you. Unfortunately, there has to be some consequences for your actions. We can't have people affiliated with the team, even in a tenuous way, gossiping to reporters. I'll talk to my family this afternoon, but I'm thinking a week-long suspension from the team facilities would be sufficient. You seem remorseful, and I'm sure something like this wouldn't happen again."

Richard seemed relieved, letting out a breath. "Thank you so much, Madeline. I definitely learned my lesson. I'm not going to be doing anything like this again, and I can't apologize enough for your family. I know you guys had nothing to do with Chris Dailey, and I'm grateful for your support of my son."

Richard and Madeline shook hands, and the two left him and his son to work out their issues. David did not seem pleased with his father. They both sat back down in the video room and it looked they were going to be embarking on a pretty heavy conversation. Davis and Madeline made their way back to the hallway to the front office area. She still felt like something was missing. They had found out who was responsible for the rumors, but still couldn't account for the person breaking into the offices or the other news stories either. Richard made sure they understood that he had only spoken to Roberts once. Could they still be running with the same story without any other corroboration? And who planted the drugs in the office in the first place? She had to talk to Jennifer Roberts. There had to be a reason she was so intent on destroying the Abington Armadillos.

Chapter Twenty

After the discussion with Richard, Madeline settled down the rest of the day at her computer and worked through several camp requests. All the local kids teams wanted to spend some time on the field with the players and learn how to hit and field like the almost pros. She was glad to see that the team was still being supported by the local community. It definitely helped ease her mind that the murder didn't cause too much strain on the team events.

She found one email sent to her but addressed to her brother. She found herself reading it before she even noticed it wasn't hers. It seemed to be some sort of apology letter.

Madeline clicked through the email to see who it was from, but there was no signature at the bottom. Looking back at the body of the email, the gist was that the person was sorry Ben got caught up in the murder investigation, and that the person knew he was innocent the whole time. Weird. The email address also looked weird. It was just a bunch of letters and numbers jumbled together with a Gmail address. Hm. Well, she wasn't going to worry about it now. She clicked forward and sent the email on to her brother's email. She knew he would be checking it even if he wasn't at the park.

There was a quick knock on the door. Madeline looked up to see her mom hovering in the doorway with an apprehensive look on her face. "Hey, Mom, do you need me for something?"

Looking over her shoulder to see if anyone was eavesdropping, she ventured into the office and shut the door behind her. Uh-oh, this could be serious. She took a seat across from Madeline's desk.

"Maddie, I wanted to talk to you privately. I realized with all the craziness of Opening Day, the murder, and the false news reports about the team, we haven't gotten to sit down and actually talk about the job you're doing here. Other than all that other stuff, are you settling in well?" She smiled.

Madeline leaned back in her chair and smiled back at her mom. Of course, she would be concerned about her daughter. They had gotten closer in the years after college, probably because she learned to appreciate her mother so much more as an adult. Of course, Madeline had gone through a few rebellious teen years and they had fought like cats and dogs back then. Now, they had a deeper relationship than most mothers and daughters. They could tell each other anything.

"I think on the business side, everything is going really well. I'm really enjoying the camp events and the team itself is doing great, too." She gave her mom a wink. "It doesn't hurt that the Red Sox are having a good season, too. It makes the summer more enjoyable. Plus, it reminds me of when Grandpa was still around."

Her mother got a wistful look on her face. "We all miss Grandpa Boucher. I married into that family, but I had known your father's parents for many years before. I even lived at their house during high school so that I wouldn't have to change schools when my family moved out of the district. He was a special guy, and he loved two things most of all. The Red Sox and family. That's why we're going to see the team through this rough patch and come out better than ever on the other side." She looked down at her hands as if collecting her thoughts. "Which brings me to the other reason I came to see you today."

Madeline sat up quickly. What else could there possibly be? Did they not like the job that she was doing? Did she mess up an interview request or something? Did it have to do with the guy canceling the first pitch ceremony? Madeline had a tendency to not think too clearly when her anxiety ramped up. It wasn't probably that serious, but she could make anything seem like the end of the world if given time.

"So, as you know, Ben had an interview with the Red Sox the day of the murder." Marie said. "I know he doesn't think he's going to get the job, but you never know. Once this whole murder thing gets cleared up, they might want to talk to him again. He'd be perfect for the job. If that's the case, your father and I wanted to approach the future of the team with you."

Madeline took a deep breath. Was she really asking her to help run the team full time? She just got back here! She hadn't had really any time to think about her future with the team before all the murder madness kicked up.

Marie continued. "I know you just came back to the team, but just think about if you'd like to take on a larger role with the front office. You've done a great job so far with the community outreach, so now would be a good time to introduce you to the business side of the team. Your father and I want to be able to retire eventually, and we would like the team to stay in the family. And we definitely don't want to leave it to your cousins. I don't think they'd love the team like we do."

Madeline must have had a shocked look on her face, because Marie just smiled at her and, "I can see I surprised you. Just take a week or so to think about it. Plus, who knows, maybe your brother will stick around and you can work side by side on the team." With that parting sentiment, she opened the door and left Madeline's office.

Wow. She never thought about staying with the team forever. Although it made sense. She wasn't really sure what to expect when she came back. The past month had been great, outside of the murder of course. The first game back and giving that kid an opportunity to meet his hero was super gratifying. She didn't remember feeling like that when she was a teenager working at the field. Now that she was older, it was more gratifying to work for a job with a tangible effect on the community. While government work was great, sometimes it felt so abstract. She never saw the end product. At the field, she saw the product every day, and frankly, it made her happy. She thought her decision might have already been made before she even started back at the field. This was the place she was meant to be. Now, to clear up the murder and get back on track this season.

Looking at the clock, she saw it was about 5 p.m., so her day could officially be over. She decided to use the time to do a bit more investigating into the people she thought were most responsible for Dailey's murder.

Starting with the people she knew, she put William Chase's name into the search bar. Up came about fifty articles about his purchase of the team and the work he was doing with the stadium to make it a state-of-the-art location. For an independent league team, he sure was spending a lot of money on upgrades. Usually teams did little things here and there to raise their profiles. Like the Abington team upgrading concessions. William Chase was planning to tear down his current stadium and try to make a mini Fenway Park on Cape Cod. She snorted. The locals must love that idea. Cape Cod was not exactly known for being a progressive place.

There didn't seem to be anything too shady about him online. He was a business guy which created some enemies, but she couldn't find any evidence of a criminal background. The next person she decided to check on was Richard Murphy. Even though she believed his feelings of remorse, it wouldn't hurt to check out his online footprint just in case. All the stories that came up were about his son and how devoted they were to each other. It confirmed what she initially thought of the Murphy family. She skipped the rest of the articles. After his apology that morning, she didn't think that Richard was involved in some grand scheme to frame her brother for murder. He seemed genuinely upset about everything that happened, and she knew that David was giving him the business about it now.

Leaning back in her char, her eye caught on the piece of paper that she picked up the other night from Dailey's girlfriend. She had some more of the names crossed off the list today, and she didn't want to revisit those names. The only other name she was really not sure about was Brittany Marks. Walter Lawson was some guy who wrote articles about the local teams. Nothing too serious there. Brittany was the mystery.

She wasn't someone Madeline knew, but obviously Ashley must have known who she was. Madeline plugged her name into the search bar and was surprised to not get any hits. Like any at all. There were a few articles about an older woman named Brittany Marche who lived in France. That obviously wasn't the one Ashley was worried about because this woman was at least eighty years old and had lived in France apparently for the past fifty years. She had no connection with Massachusetts or baseball at all.

She saw Davis enter her office out of the corner of her eye. He sat down across from her. "You looked deep in thought a minute ago. I hope it doesn't have anything to do with investigating Dailey's murder. Your brother is finally cleared, the rumors will start dying down, and it's time to let it go."

Sighing, she said. "I know I should probably let it go. But now it's just curiosity. This whole thing has had such a major effect on my family and the team I want to make sure there are no more surprises. And on that note, I did find another interesting thing. I was looking through the names on this list that Dailey's girlfriend dropped and found a name that I can't find any information about. Brittany Marks. The only thing that came back on the internet was some old lady in France. Don't you find that odd?" She looked at Davis hoping he would see the weirdness of her situation and pointed at her computer screen as she turned it towards him.

He sort of rolled his eyes and leaned forward to see what she pulled up. "Maddie, that is weird, but we don't know why his girlfriend had that list. Maybe it was a list of people to invite to a party and just happened to include people who might have murdered her boyfriend. It is weird that there would be an eighty-year-old French woman on the list, but not completely out of the realm of possibility.

"Okay, well fine. I still think it's weird. The guy was a bad dude, and all the names on this list have some sort of connection with him that should be looked at closely. Has Detective Stephenson even talked to any of these people? And if I couldn't find a local Brittany Marks, would he find the right person?" Madeline pondered.

Davis chuckled as he got up out of his seat. "Well, he is actually trained for this kind of work, so I'm sure he has taken all the information you so luckily found and put it through the investigation wringer. This isn't your fight anymore, Maddie." Pausing at the door, he turned one more time. "Oh, we're on our way over to Centerfields for Happy Hour. You in?"

Madeline nodded and started to shut down her computer system. "I'll meet you guys over there in about ten minutes. I want to finish up some paperwork before I leave." He flicked his fingers in acknowledgment. After she saw he left the office towards the restaurant, she grabbed at the suspect list and shoved it into her purse. She was definitely going to get to the bottom of the mystery person. It had to have something to do with the murder. There wasn't any other logical explanation.

Chapter Twenty-One

It was only 6 p.m. on a Sunday afternoon, but Centerfields was hopping. Unfortunately, bars in Massachusetts weren't technically allowed to have "happy hour" specials due to some blue laws, but many bars got around that by offering all day specials. For being such a progressive state, there were still puritanical laws on the books that for some reason, never got repealed. They also had decently priced glasses of wine, which was Madeline's sweet spot.

Spotting the security group, Davis among them, she wound her way through the crush of people near the bar. The Red Sox game was scheduled for that night on the national channel, and it looked like a lot of people had gotten to the bar early to stake out a seat to watch the game. She saw that the security team was in a corner of the bar with a TV set up right next to the table. They definitely wouldn't be missing the game that night. Walking up to the team, she waved at Esther who was talking to one of the guys who worked parking lot security on game days. She excused herself from the conversation and made her way over to Madeline.

"Hey, Maddie! I'm so glad you came tonight. Davis told me all about your investigations of the murder in order to clear your brother. You must be glad he finally got released from the police." Hugging Madeline, she pulled her towards one of the bar stools they had reserved. Madeline waved at the waitress, who was the usual one and she nodded. She already knew Madeline's order before she even had to say anything.

"I don't know if he's fully clear yet, just that the police have realized they don't have much to hold him on now. Especially since Ben finally came clean about his alibi." Madeline wasn't sure if he wanted everyone to know about the job interview, so she left it at that, and Esther didn't pry.

Madeline sat at the bar and turned to face Esther. "And well, I wouldn't say I'm done looking into it. I found a name that I'm curious about and wondering how it fits into this whole mess. Davis isn't too happy that I'm still looking into it, but I just can't let it go. It's my family. It's my team." She looked around and saw Davis looking at her huddled with Esther. Esther followed her eyes and saw Davis looking over. She gave him a wave and turned back towards Madeline.

"You know, Maddie, it might not be my place, but I think he really likes you. He's talking about your safety in some of our security briefing meetings in the mornings. Since the investigation is ongoing, he wants to make sure you're safe since the murder and the break-in. I can't say I blame him either. I mean, two very dramatic things have happened to you in the past few weeks, not even counting the murder." Esther looked at her and patted Madeline's arm. "We all just want to keep you and your family safe."

The waitress returned at that moment with Madeline's glass of wine and a beer for Esther. They decided to order some nachos and head over for a quick game of pool. The Red Sox were warming up with batting practice on TV, and the security team was ready to let loose after a crazy baseball week. Esther and Madeline teamed up against some of the security guys, including Davis. Madeline knew she had an ace up her sleeve; Esther was a crack pool shark. She hustled guys in college for extra beer money by going to various pool halls and playing the young innocent college students. Some nights she left with over $100 of winnings. Madeline wasn't sure if the security guys knew, but they were about to lose and lose bad.

After two quick games of pool, Madeline excused herself to the bathroom. The impromptu happy hour was turning into a super fun event. The whole security team was cool, and no one really treated her like the bosses' daughter, which she was worried about when she came back. Taking her phone with her so she could check her text messages, she pushed open the door and took one of the unoccupied stalls. Before she could leave the stall, the door opened to the bathroom and two women walked in talking fast and furiously.

"What do you mean they're still investigating? I thought you said you took care of it?" one high-pitched voice hissed angrily.

"I did. It's not my fault that this family is like Teflon. Nothing seems to stick to them. The drug thing worked for a bit. I just need to get more dirt and then I can do something." The other voice was low and sounded like the person was trying to calm the other one down.

Madeline tried to peek through the space in the bathroom door to see who the voices belonged to. Unfortunately, both women were just out of sight. She tried jamming her face closer to the door in hopes she could catch a glimpse, but instead her phone fell out of her hand and clattered to the floor. She heard both women suck in a breath and quickly scramble out the door. Madeline tried to follow, but the stall door lock got stuck. Swearing, she scrambled to unlock the door, but she knew she wouldn't see the two ladies who were there.

Madeline ran out the bathroom door and looked around. The bar was so crowded; there was no way she could pick out the two women. She should've looked closer at their shoes. Then maybe she could identify them. Man, it would've been nice if she could've caught the gossipers.

Madeline sighed and headed back to the table with the security group. Davis motioned her over to where he and Esther were deep in conversation. As she approached the table, she heard her name over the cacophony of the crowded room. Madeline turned in a circle and could just barely make out Tom's head above the crowd making his way over. She waved him over to join the group. Davis' lips tightened as Tom approached. She introduced the two men and there was an awkward handshake. Both men stood up tall, as if taking measure of each other. The tension was definitely palpable.

Esther must have felt it too, because she quickly diverted attention to the fact that the Red Sox were up 2–0 in the bottom of the second inning. "Hey! Look at that, the ace is dealing tonight!"

"Hey, Tom," Madeline said. "What are you doing out here tonight? Got any big scouting plans?"

He laughed and looked around the bar. "Not exactly. I was supposed to meet a former college player here for a drink and talk about some future options, but he never showed up." He shrugged. "Then I saw you and thought I'd come over and say hi now that things look to be calming down a bit."

Madeline laughed, her go-to move to avoid awkwardness. She looked over at Davis who had a frown on his face as he studied his beer. Turning her attention back to Tom, she wanted to let him know that she appreciated his help in the past few days. "Tom, I wanted to thank you for helping me out this week. Finding out more about the victim and William Chase really helped us put things in perspective. I don't know if anyone is closer to finding out who the murderer actually is, but that's not my job anyway, right?"

"No problem. Anything to help you and your family. You guys have always been good to me the past few years, so it's the least I could do to pay you guys back. Speaking of your family"—he leaned forward—"I heard through the grapevine that your brother is going to work for the big guys. The Sox."

She must have looked shocked, because he quickly continued. "I mean, that's just the rumor going around. I don't even know if it's true."

Madeline schooled her face to make a neutral expression. "Well, I guess the cat is out of the bag. Sort of anyway. He did have an interview, but he's still waiting for them to make a decision before he makes a decision. If that makes sense." She waved a hand in the air. "The family understands completely though. I mean, it's the Red Sox! It's the dream! So, no worries at this point." She tried to smile, but still had some doubts about what Ben's leaving might mean to the family and the team.

A raucous cheer went up from the bar; the Red Sox designated hitter hammered a homerun to drive in two more runs. Even though it was only June, any time the team started to go on a streak, the fan base tended to get wicked excited. Luckily, her grandpa was still around when the Red Sox won their championship in 2004. That was a memory that she'd never forget. The 86-year curse was broken, and her grandpa couldn't have been happier. They watched the final game as a family, and when Keith Foulke tossed the ball to first base for the last out, they all stood and cheered. There were tears and screaming. Since then, the team had won a bunch more championships, each one sweeter than the last. But nothing would ever replicate that first one, though.

She shook herself out of her baseball memories and took another look around the bar to see if anyone else looked familiar. In the far corner of the bar, she caught a glimpse of long blonde hair that seemed familiar. Turning around in her seat to get a better look, she could've sworn it was Jennifer Roberts, the reporter. She guessed it wasn't completely out of the ordinary to see her in the bar, but she still got an uneasy feeling. She didn't think that Jennifer noticed her watching her; she kept looking at her watch and then at the front door of the restaurant. Madeline felt a tap on her shoulder and saw Davis standing over her following the direction of her eyes towards Jennifer.

"Hey, did you see Jennifer over there?" Davis pointed into the darkness of the bar.

"Yeah, I guess I was just wondering what she was doing here again. I don't think I've ever seen her at this bar before she confronted us, and then she didn't even stay that long. I guess she could just be here getting a drink, but it looks like she's waiting for someone." She looked back at Davis. "Oh! I did overhear two women in the bathroom talking about drugs and the rumors. I couldn't see who was talking, but I wonder if she is involved. I mean, she does have some sort of vendetta towards the family, at least that's how it seems the past few weeks. It's not completely out of the realm of possibility that she was involved."

"You can't go around half-cocked just accusing people of things though. We don't know if Richard Murphy was her only lead regarding the rumors or if she's involved any more than that. I say we just sit and wait a bit. She seems to be waiting for someone, let's see who shows up." Davis put a hand on her shoulder.

Madeline felt a quick zip of electricity where he touched her. Not the static electricity kind, but the kind a person gets from someone they have chemistry with. She tried to look at him out of the corner of her eye to see if he had the same reaction she did, and she saw him look down at his hand and quickly pull it off her shoulder. They both looked away from each other and looked anywhere but at each other. Madeline cleared her throat and stepped away.

Tom pretended not to notice the awkwardness between Madeline and Davis. This was a nightmare for her. The guy she was kind of dating and the other guy she had a crush on for most of her adult life. Tom put his head closer to hers to be heard over the crowd.

"Hey, is everything okay? I heard you telling Davis about Jennifer Roberts. You guys went to high school together, right? She's trying to break into national news I think. She tried to badger me for comments on the murder last week, but I gave her the brush off."

She was only half listening to him at that point, because Jennifer hopped off the stool she was on at the bar and made her way towards the bathroom. Madeline saw her glance over at Ashley and give an almost imperceptible nod to the door. Jennifer went into the ladies' room. Ashley stood for a few seconds, looking around, and then followed her in.

"Davis! Did you see that?" He looked at her then looked around the room.

"No, what are you talking about?"

Tom was looking around also trying to determine what she was so animated about.

"Jennifer Roberts, the reporter, and Ashley, Dailey's girlfriend, just met in the bathroom. Why do they know each other? That's suspicious, right? And how are they both connected to William? That night at the bar both women seemed to be talking to him."

Both guys looked at her as if she was crazy. Maybe she was. Maybe she was just seeing suspicious things everywhere. It just felt odd that for those two different people to be suddenly meeting each other in such a public place associated with the Abington team. There was also the nod that she saw Jennifer give to Ashley before they headed to the bathroom. That sure looked like a secret communication to her.

"Esther, can you casually go into the bathroom and see what those two ladies are talking about? Or if they're talking at all? Maybe it's just a coincidence, but I don't buy it. I can't be the one to go over there; they both know me already. Jennifer is already annoyed at me because I won't give her a salacious story for her news reports."

Esther rolled her eyes and put her beer down. "Okay, but you owe me. This is kind of weird." She took off towards the ladies' room shaking her head.

Another cheer went up from the bar crowd as the Red Sox scored again. While she was excited the team was winning, she was distracted by staring at the bathroom door waiting for information. Esther came back out less than a minute later shaking her head. Not two seconds after Esther, Jennifer came out, looked around, and made her way to the exit, grabbing her keys from her purse as she walked.

Ashley was last to leave the bathroom, and seemed a little bit distracted. When she saw Madeline looking at her, her face looked shocked. Eyes wide, mouth open, and Madeline could clearly hear her swear and turn towards the exit. She scampered out the door behind Jennifer before Madeline could even move. Esther arrived back at the group after pushing her way through the happy baseball fans.

"Maddie that was a waste of time. As soon as I opened the door both women stopped talking, made like they were washing their hands, so I left. As you saw, they left right after me. I didn't even hear them talking to each other. While I was in there, they didn't even acknowledge each other." Esther took a swig of her beer. "I think you're just being a bit paranoid, Maddie. Those two aren't smart enough to be colluding on anything. What could they have to talk about anyway? And on that secret spy note, I have to get home. I want to be there before the kids go to bed."

Esther gave me a quick hug and before letting go, leaned into Madeline's ear. "Girl, you got two guys here. I think both of them are digging on you. Don't drag it out too long." Squeezing her arm one last time, Esther grabbed her bag off the table and left the restaurant.

Madeline looked over at the two guys standing awkwardly at the bar table together. Both were looking serious and watching the TV. Looking at the two guys standing together, Madeline realized how similar they actually were. Both were decent guys with decent jobs and seemed to like her.

Davis was her schoolgirl crush. She wondered if that's where her feelings were coming in. On the other hand, Tom was someone completely new. He seemed nice and already had her mom's stamp of approval. Of course, Davis did too. Madeline had to say, both men were great but at that moment, she had way too much going on to worry about her love life. Any big decisions would have to wait until Chris Dailey's murderer was caught and the rumors swirling around the team died down.

After an uncomfortable silence watching the game, Tom looked over at Madeline. "Well, I guess I'd better head out. Got a long day at the club tomorrow to get ready for. Are you free next week for another coffee date?"

Glancing over at Davis, she saw he was playing with the label of his beer. Turning back to Tom, she said, "Sure, just shoot me a text or call when you're free. We have a few day camps coming this week, but I can work around some of that." He leaned in awkwardly and gave her a quick hug. Nodding, he turned and left her and Davis alone in the restaurant.

"So…" She trailed off and tried to think of something else to say.

"Well," Davis said at the same time. They smiled at each other.

Madeline took a quick look at her watch and realized how late it was getting. She was not the type to stay out late drinking, especially on a school night. She knew it was time to pack it in. All the excitement of seeing Jennifer and Ashley together wore off, and now she was just as confused as ever. It seemed there were a few puzzle pieces that didn't fit with each other. She knew it wasn't her place to put the puzzle together, but she needed to see it through. She couldn't leave all the loose ends around that could potentially ensnare her family in the future.

"Davis, I'm going to head out," she said, placing her hand on his arm.

"Okay, I'm going to stay and watch some more of the game. Text me to let me know you made it safely." Davis gave her a smile. "And try not to think too much about what you saw tonight. It could all be completely innocent."

As she left the bar, she kept thinking about the two women's voices she heard in the bathroom. Could one of the voices have been Jennifer? She had had it out for her family since the story broke. She also wondered why she couldn't quite remember her from high school. She went to a big school, but faces were usually easy to remember. Madeline made a resolution to find her high school yearbook when she arrived home that night to do some research. At least that was some useful piece of research that would at least answer one or two questions.

Chapter Twenty-Two

Madeline woke up the next morning with a twinge of a headache. It wasn't that she drank too much the night before, but it was probably just an amalgamation of the stress of the past few weeks combined with wine. Hangovers were not something that usually happened to her, she was lucky that way. Not that she was a big drinker to begin with. She stretched in bed, kicking one of the cats off the bed by accident. Even though they couldn't talk back, she spent the next few minutes apologizing profusely. Having mad cats was not something she needed to add to her plate.

Thankfully it was Monday. There was nothing pressing to deal with at the park since the next games weren't scheduled until the following weekend. She decided to take the morning to get some things done at home that she had been neglecting the past few weeks. Before she could do that, she really wanted to satisfy the curiosity she had about Jennifer Roberts. She still didn't remember her from any classes in high school, but it was a long time ago. Lord knows she had changed, maybe Jennifer did too.

After a quick breakfast of cinnamon toast and iced tea, she put on the boy bands radio station and headed into the basement to find her old yearbooks. She was sort of a pack rat, so all four years of high school yearbooks were kept in a plastic tub. Also in the tubs were here mementos of her younger life. Like the time she went to Europe with a choral group to sing across the continent, or pieces of jewelry from homecoming dances. She had been lucky enough not to have a bad experience in high school. She straddled the line between loser and cool kids. The choir nerds and the cool kids who played sports both accepted her. She lucked out.

Pulling the gray tub from behind a wall of boxes, she lugged it upstairs and put it down on the living room floor, sending a cloud of dust into her face. She coughed and opened the tub to see what goodies she could find. The three cats joined her as they explored the new object in their midst. Right on top was a set of four hardbound yearbooks. She probably didn't need to buy one for each year, but the yearbook team had a way of convincing gullible students that they needed a yearbook each year to round out their high school experience.

Madeline pulled out her senior yearbook and flipped to the senior pictures. She hated hers. She had bangs and some god-awful gold sweater on. She didn't know what she was thinking. She guessed she could chalk it up to late 90s fashion, but it was almost the year 2000 when her picture was taken; she should've known better. Whatever.

She flipped several pages to the "R" section. Running her finger along the pictures and the names, she didn't see anyone listed with the name Roberts, let alone Jennifer. She wondered if that was her married name. Maybe that's why she couldn't find her. Madeline flipped back to the front of the senior section and went page by page.

Still nothing.

Closing the yearbook, she texted Esther to see if she had any ideas about Jennifer at all. While Madeline waited for a response, she wondered if something deeper was going on. Did Jennifer actually attend her high school or was she just trying to ingratiate herself with her to get a juicy story? But why lie about something that could be easily verified? Of course, Madeline had taken two weeks to check on an obviously sketchy story to begin with, so maybe it wasn't that crazy of an idea.

Madeline's phone pinged and she saw Esther had responded. She couldn't remember anyone with that name from high school either, and when they were at the bar the night before she didn't recognize her. Esther knew everyone in school. She was one of the popular crowd and made it her mission to know everyone. If she didn't remember Jennifer, then there were definitely some shenanigans going on.

Putting the yearbooks back into their gray container, she turned up her wireless speakers and began to clean the house. It was rare she had a morning off to herself, so getting the housework done was necessary. The cats chased her around as she ran the vacuum cleaner, and attacked her feet as she cleaned the litterboxes. They also had their habits when she did her chores. She was jamming out to an old *NSYNC song, waving around her feather duster, when she heard a ping from her phone.

Madeline ran over to her phone and saw a text message from a number she didn't know. She opened it warily, hoping that it didn't have some virus or something attached to it. It was a brief message:

Maddie, we need to talk. Meet me at the Barnstable Barnstormers stadium today at 5pm. ALONE! — William

She couldn't believe first that William finagled her phone number somehow, let alone that he would text her to talk. She remembered when he accosted her at Opening Day, but she thought he got the answers he was looking for already because she hadn't heard from him. Why her? If he was looking for some back-channel communication for information regarding the team, he really picked the wrong person. Madeline only knew the basics and was still learning; she hadn't even made any front office decisions without checking with multiple people.

She mulled over the situation. She really wanted to find out what he wanted to talk to her about. Maddie decided that it couldn't hurt to make a trip out in the afternoon to see what he wanted. Even though she had a momentary feeling of unease, seeing that he was still a possible suspect on her list of Dailey's murderers, her overwhelming need to find out what was up overrode that.

She wasn't crazy though. She wouldn't just go there alone without letting someone know where she was going. Also, it would be good to have some back-up just in case.

Madeline dashed off a quick message to Davis and her brother, letting them know where she was going. She knew they wouldn't have wanted her to go out by herself, but the afternoon was fast approaching and she didn't want to waste time. Plus, she thought it was relatively safe since it was early enough in the evening to still be light out. Nothing too bad could happen to her in the daytime. She made sure she had her cell phone and grabbed a little can of mace that she used when she was in the city. One could never be too careful.

Since it was summer, the days extended into early evening and the sun didn't set until well after 8 p.m. It was going to be broad daylight, and she didn't get the sense that William wanted to hurt her. She didn't have any proof that he was involved in the murder, just had some connections with the victim. She'd be fine. Nothing to worry about.

An hour after she texted Davis, she pulled into the Barnstormers parking lot. There were a few cars in the lot, but there didn't seem to be too many people out and about. She knew the team had a game that week, one of the only teams to play during the week as well as weekends. Lots of tourists in the summer made the Barnstormers team invaluable to the local economy. She would've thought there would be more hustle and bustle so close to game days. Then again, she didn't know how the owner and manager ran their team; maybe they just did things differently. As a newbie to the industry, she probably shouldn't judge too harshly.

She still hadn't heard back from Davis yet, but checking her email she saw another email from Esther. It confirmed what she said earlier about not going to school with Jennifer Roberts or anyone who looked like her. She must have been faking the connection to try and get more information from Madeline regarding the team and her family. As if she would know any more than the public knew about the investigation.

With that mystery solved, she took a deep breath and made her way to the front office door. There wasn't any movement at the front desk, which provoked a sigh of relief from her. She just wasn't sure she could've faced the old battle axe receptionist that day. The past few weeks had been so stressful, and she didn't need that woman's attitude to pile it on. She tried the door handle and found it opened easily under her hand.

"Hello? Is anyone here? Mr. Chase?" She cautiously entered the offices. Most of the doors were shut tight, and the only light was coming from the windows behind her. Slowly stepping around the receptionist desk and peering down the hallway, she tried one more time.

"Mr. Chase? It's Madeline Boucher. You wanted to meet with me?"

She heard a small groan from the last office. William Chase's office. She ran down the small hallway and found his door ajar. Pushing it open, she found William lying on the floor clutching his head. Blood seeped through his fingers and his eyes were closed tightly. The office was a mess. Papers were strewn about the floor and his desk. His baseball memorabilia was tossed around and the glass from picture frames was shattered all on the floor.

Madeline ran to William's side and pulled out her cellphone.

"Don't worry, William, I'm calling an ambulance right now. You'll be okay."

His eyes opened and looked at her unfocusedly. They were glazed over and she wasn't even sure if he knew who she was or what she said. Madeline gave the nice dispatcher on the other end of the phone all her information and promised to stay on the line until help showed up. While she waited to hear the sounds of sirens, she took another moment to look around the room closer. What a mess. Someone must have been looking for something pretty important to cause such chaos.

William grasped her free hand and pulled her down towards him. "My daughter." Those words were all he said before he promptly passed out.

Daughter? She didn't know William had a family. He never mentioned it in the press, and he sure as heck didn't act like a settled down man. She looked around the office again to see if there was anything to confirm what he just said. Madeline saw a tiny silver frame peeking out from the corner of his desk. She didn't want to touch anything, but she could see a child's face and moved closer. It was a blonde girl, about four years old, holding William's hand. That must be his daughter. She wondered why he wanted her to know about the girl. And who was the mother? Why the big secret about his family?

She made her way back to his side and hoped he had regained consciousness. "William, what do you mean about your daughter? Is she in danger? Who is the mother?" She leaned over his prone body and tried to get a response, but he was still out cold.

As she pondered the new information, the paramedics and police burst through the office door. They started to attend to William right away and the police ushered her out of the office to a waiting Detective Stephenson. Shaking his head, he pulled her out the front door to the parking lot.

"Madeline, I admit. When they called me and said Madeline Boucher called in an assault victim in Barnstable, I was surprised. It was out of my jurisdiction, but the local police chief and I are friends, so he gave me a call when he heard your name. He's been keeping me in the loop about the Barnstable team. I have been in touch with him about William Chase for a while now. But the real question is, what were you doing here today?"

"Look, I know it seems weird. But William sent me a text this morning asking me to meet him here. I can show you the message." She fished her phone out of her pocket and thrust it in the detective's face. "See! I was just meeting him to discuss something. When I got here, no one answered at the front desk and I heard a groan from the back office. That's when I found him."

He nodded as he jotted things down in his notepad. "Fine, wait here for a moment. I'm going to check on things.

Madeline tapped her foot impatiently as she waited for the detective to return. Her mind swirled with questions about the attack and if it was connected to Christopher Dailey at all.

The Detective returned a few minutes later and guided her to a bench near the front entrance. "First of all, the medics say William will be fine. Just a nasty concussion. Hopefully he'll be able to remember his attacker. Second, I see from the text message that he wanted to talk to you. Do you have any idea of what it was about?"

She squirmed under his gaze. She didn't think he knew that she had been continuing to investigate behind his back. She didn't want him to yell at her. "Well, I'm not one hundred percent sure, to be honest. A few weeks ago, he had cornered me at the Abington ballpark to say that we needed to talk, but I got pulled away. This is the first time he's reached out to me since then. I assume it had something to do with the murder investigation. With all the rumors going around and whatnot, he must have had something to tell me. Why else would he contact me?"

"That what we have to figure out." The detective looked at her closely. "Did he say anything to you before he lost consciousness?"

Madeline wasn't sure what was important and what wasn't important anymore. Did William actually call her to his office to tell her something about the murder? Did he know something about the rumors being spread about the Armadillos? Was it something else entirely? And who was his daughter? Who was her mother? The questions swirled around in her head until it made sort of a muddled soup. She didn't know how to make heads or tails of the situation anymore. She kept finding more questions and not getting any more answers.

Before she could respond to the detective's question, there was a screech of tires in the parking lot and she looked up to see Davis' black SUV tear into the lot. He frantically put the car in park and looked towards the entrance. Detective Stephenson waved him over.

"I took the liberty of informing Davis that you had called 911. Since he's been involved in the investigation and helping us out, I thought he would have liked to know that you were okay."

Madeline didn't tell the detective that she already informed Davis where she was going to be. He would've heard about this whole situation anyway. She was oddly touched that both men seemed to be concerned with her well-being. Davis approached her and the detective with a quickness that surprised her.

"Maddie! Are you okay? I literally just read your text when the detective called me. Is William okay? Did you get hurt?" He awkwardly held out his hands as if to engulf her in a hug, but quickly dropped them and ran a hand through his hair.

As he asked the questions, the paramedics wheeled the stretcher bearing William out the front door towards the waiting ambulance. William seemed to be still passed out, and the paramedics let the detective know they were taking him to Cape Cod Hospital for further observation. His injuries didn't seem life threatening to them, but since he hadn't regained consciousness yet, they wanted to keep monitoring him at least overnight.

"Well, since this is outside my jurisdiction, I'll get back over the bridge. If you have any other information Madeline, please call me. Anything at all. No more running off without letting someone know what's going on. You've had threats sent to you and there is still a murderer running around. Don't forget about that." Detective Stephenson sauntered back to his waiting unmarked car after pausing to talk to the local police.

Madeline stood there awkwardly with Davis. Clearing her throat, she said, "Thanks for coming down, Davis. I just wish I knew what he had wanted to talk to me about. I wish I could've talked to him more before he passed out. He seemed insistent that he had something important to tell me."

She thought for a moment, staring out into the now quiet parking lot. "Oh! He did say one weird thing though. I meant to tell the detective, but things got crazy there for a minute."

"What did he say?" Davis asked.

"Something about his daughter. And I saw a small picture broken on the ground of a little girl that might have been who he was talking about. I didn't even know he had a daughter or a family, did you?"

Davis rubbed his chin and then shook his head. "I didn't really know all that much about him to begin with. But he certainly didn't seem or act like a devoted family guy. And he never wore a wedding ring, so I would've assumed he was unmarried. When he became owner of the team there would have been profiles of his life outside of baseball, and I definitely don't remember family ever being mentioned."

Madeline wondered why William would keep the secret of a family or a daughter. Then again, she hadn't gone out of her way to learn about him too much, so maybe it wasn't an active secret. Maybe other people knew. He was still on her list of people to find out more about, but she hadn't done a deep dive on him yet. She made a mental note to check out what she could find on the good old internet when she got home.

"Are you going to be okay driving home?" Davis asked.

"Of course, finding William Chase alive is much less scary than finding a dead body. I'm going to just head back home to hunker down for the night. The plans for the team later this week are going to take a lot of energy that I should probably rest up for." She didn't tell him that she was also going to start diving into the William Chase and his daughter mystery. If she found anything important, that's when she'd tell him.

Chapter Twenty-Three

Madeline's three cats wound themselves around her feet when she arrived home later that night. After all the rigmarole at the Barnstable stadium, she didn't get back to her house until a bit after 8 p.m. She didn't fool herself that her cats were really glad she was home, but rather they were just really glad she was home so they could be fed. She popped open some wet food cans, placed them on the floor, and walked to her bedroom shedding her clothes.

The air conditioner was running full blast due to the summer-like temperatures that had been creeping up the last few weeks. That meant her house was a veritable ice chest. She made it to the bedroom and bundled up in her college sweatpants and a Red Sox hoodie. She pulled her computer from its place next to her bed and logged on. She needed to find out about William's mystery family. It was causing her Spidey sense to begin tingling and she couldn't ignore it. There were too many questions piling up and she needed to find some things out.

First, there was learning about the familial connection between William Chase and Christopher Dailey. Then, there was the whole thing about William trying to get in contact with her so many times. That was definitely worth exploring in and of itself. Did the person who attacked William know that he had contacted her that day? It was just all so suspicious. Either he knew something about the murder that he wanted to tell her about, or he knew exactly who the culprit is. Either way, before passing out he had referenced a mysterious daughter so I had to start digging.

She knew that it was getting late, but she needed to use the opportunity while things were fresh in her mind. Madeline pulled up Google and typed William's name in the search bar. Luckily, he was one of the main hits after she included the word "Barnstable" in the search. She clicked on the images button and he was all over the site. She scrolled through a bunch of pictures of him, by himself, at different business functions in the area. Nothing immediately suspicious or even remotely to do with his family jumped out so she continued to the second page of pictures.

There!

She rubbed her eyes, not sure if it was the eyestrain from being so late, or if she was actually looking at a picture of William with Jennifer Roberts and Chris Dailey together at some event. She pulled the computer closer to her face, clicked on the image, and opened the page. It was a notice about a fundraiser held in the city for some local charity over five years ago. The caption read, "Local businessman William Chase poses with girlfriend, Jessica Jenkins, and friend, Christopher Dailey."

Jessica Jenkins, not Roberts? Girlfriend? That was definitely a picture of Jennifer Roberts as Madeline knew her in the picture. She did a quick Facebook search on Jessica Jenkins and found her right away. The profile hadn't been active for over three years, and it seemed like she dropped off the earth after that. There weren't any other sites for her, outside of her media page for the news. She was a social media ghost privately, which was hard to do in that day and age. Digging deeper into the old profile, she found another picture of her with Chris Dailey. They were hanging out on some beach together, and the caption read, "Having a great time on vacation!"

Madeline sat back in her bed rubbing her temples and tried to sort out the new information. So, wait. Did she date Chris and then William? And they were all friends at one time? Were they still all friends? This just kept getting weirder and weirder. And did it have something to do with the murder or attack on William? She typed in the website of the local TV station to see if they had some sort of biography on Jennifer Roberts. Or Jessica. Whatever she called herself.

Pulling up the profiles of their "on-air talent" pages, she found Jennifer on the bottom of the list under "new" talent. She clicked on the picture of the heavily made-up Jennifer and scanned the bio they had for her. It was pretty sparse. It had mentioned her arriving from down south to report on local news for the channel. No mention of family, friends, or any other personal information.

Madeline took a minute to collect her thoughts, looked at the clock, and gasped. It was already one a.m.! She needed to get some sleep before work the next day. Now that she was older, staying up late hurt a lot more than when she was in her twenties. Her friends always joked that she was an eighty-year-old woman in a thirty-year-old body. Saving the pages of both Jessica and Jennifer that she found, she logged off the computer and burrowed under her covers. Sleep for now, investigation for tomorrow.

Chapter Twenty-Four

Unfortunately, with all the thoughts swirling around in Madeline's head, sleep did not come easily. She tossed and turned most of the night and ended up with only four hours of uninterrupted sleep by the time her alarm rang at 7 a.m. She groaned and stretched, startling the cats on the bed. Lack of sleep was not going to be an asset today, not if she wanted to get to the bottom of the Jessica/Jennifer/Chris debacle that she found out about last night.

She showered, ran a blow dryer through her hair, put on a team baseball cap, and waltzed out the door in about half an hour. Before she left, she sent a quick text message to Davis letting him know the most recent drama she found out about last night.

Hey Davis, Jennifer Roberts isn't who she says she is. I'll tell you more at the office.

Madeline needed a caffeine jolt, so she stopped at the Dunkin' Donuts down the street from the ballpark. Once she arrived at the ballpark, she enjoyed the sense of calm the early morning provided. Or at least, it provided a sense of calm until she started thinking about the murder again. She saw only two other cars in the parking lot belonging to the field crew, so she knew she'd have the place to herself for a while. She walked into the front office, threw her purse down on her desk chair, and walked towards the tunnel to the field.

It was still early enough that the players hadn't reported yet for practice. During the week there were voluntary practices at the beginning of the week for the games on the weekends. Some of the players had other part time jobs outside of the game since it was not as highly paid as the pros. The team had mandatory practices Thursdays and Fridays all day on game weeks since most of the games were on the weekend. Tuesday was a notorious dead time at the park. Even now, there were only a few groundskeepers out on the field trimming up the outfield and raking the infield dirt.

The field looked pretty good considering the fact the last game was played just a few days previously. Madeline waved at Dave as he watered the pitcher's mound. This time of the day was great to just enjoy the park. She sighed and turned away from the field to head back to her office. Making the quick trek, she found that the corridor in her office was still quiet.

Her parents and brother all arrived around the same time, usually about an hour after she arrived. Davis was usually in early like she was, so she found it odd that he hadn't arrived yet. That, and he hadn't responded to her text yet either. She thought the Jennifer/Jessica information was pretty mind-blowing and possibly super important. She must've been involved with Chris. In that picture she found online they looked pretty close. Add that to the fact they were allegedly, possibly dating at one time, her now all up in the Abington Armadillos business couldn't be a coincidence.

Madeline sat behind her computer, trying to focus on her emails when she heard Eliza open the front door and fling her giant purse on her desk.

"Anyone home?" she called from the front desk.

Madeline poked her head out of her office and gave Eliza a wave. Eliza dashed towards her office and pulled the door closed behind her. "I know there are voicemails waiting for me, but I need to hear from the horse's mouth what happened at the Barnstable Stadium between you and William Chase yesterday!"

"How did you hear about that already?" Madeline smiled at Eliza. "Wait, let me guess. The administrative assistant grapevine started with his lovely assistant and spread to you before daybreak this morning?" She shrugged and gave her a smile. "Yeah, that's what I thought. Nothing scandalous happened. He texted that he wanted to meet. I went, and I found him on the floor of his office, knocked out."

Swiveling around in her chair, Madeline stopped to think more about what actually happened the day before. Was he attacked because someone knew he was meeting with her to tell her about the murder? Was she overthinking everything? Maybe it was supposed to be an innocuous business meeting. He had been trying to get in touch with her ever since she started back at the park. Of course, now that she found out about a connection between him and the fake Jennifer Roberts, she had a million more questions.

Madeline leaned towards Eliza. She decided to tell her everything, to see if she had any other insights. "I think there is something going on with Jennifer Roberts and William Chase. He mentioned a daughter. What if she's the mother and was still involved with Chris Dailey on the side?" She quickly filled Eliza in about what she found out via her internet searches the night before.

"Dang. That's ten ways of crazy. It's like a soap opera. And you think this Jennifer/Jessica person might be ultimately responsible for Dailey's death?" Eliza asked the sixty-four-thousand-dollar question.

Madeline thought for a minute. Did she think that Jennifer/Jessica had a hand in the murder? "Maybe. I mean, I don't know. It just seems odd that she appeared so suddenly in our lives after the murder and has made it her life's mission to throw my family under the bus for everything. Maybe she is trying to deflect suspicion. Obviously, it must have worked a bit because I haven't heard of anyone else being arrested. Plus, they keep talking to my brother instead of looking elsewhere."

Eliza got a serious look on her face. She checked to make sure the door was still closed tightly and leaned forward over the desk. Madeline leaned forwards as well until they were close over the top of the desk.

"I think we should set up a sting. We should invite her to the park to see if we can get her to confess that she's William's baby mama. At the very least, we can try to solve that mystery." She winked at Madeline and got up to head back to her desk.

It did seem like a crazy idea, but then again, what harm could a nosy reporter cause her? Other than reporting lies about her family, of course. She already caused Madeline enough stress with her reporting. Maybe she could try to get Jennifer on her side to find out more information about Chris and William.

The only thing to figure out was a way to get her to talk to Madeline. Until she could figure out a way to do that, there was still some real baseball work to do. First on her list was pulling together an Instagram contest for fans to win swag and tickets for upcoming games. Her bright idea also included sending the mascot of the team out to local landmarks on the South Shore to interact with the community. Peaceful Meadows Ice Cream in Whitman, Wollaston Beach in Quincy, and the Hanover Mall were all on the lists of places for the Armadillo to hit in the next few weeks.

Madeline finished up a call with a local little league organization about bringing the Armadillos mascot to their tournament in the next few weeks. The kids loved seeing Arnold the Armadillo out of the ballpark. Her grandfather used to tell a story that Ben and she were terrified of the mascot as a kid. It used to be more realistic, but it scared too many young kids. They redesigned it to more resemble a cartoon character. Less crying children at the ballpark was always a good idea. She finalized the dates and times with the team and started to pull tighter the marketing materials for the upcoming ticket contests that she wanted to hold.

Before she knew it, it was late afternoon and found that she had worked straight through lunch. She didn't even notice the rest of the family had come in for the workday. Davis hadn't even stopped by. She stood up, stretched her arms behind her back, and made her way to her mom's office. When she arrived there, the door was open; her mom was on the phone and held up one finger, indicating to wait. Madeline sat in the chair across from her to wait while she finished up the call.

"Yes, thanks, Denise. We'll get together later to discuss terms of the sponsorship. I appreciate your contribution to the team for the upcoming games and the rest of the season." With a quick goodbye, she hung up the phone. She gave Madeline a stern look and came around the desk to sit next to her.

"Now, what's this I hear about you getting caught up in a mess over in Barnstable?"

Madeline quickly filled her in on the latest updates and shenanigans by all the players in the investigation. She nodded as Madeline told her about the surprise revelation that Jennifer Roberts was not who she claimed to be. She sat back with a thoughtful look on her face.

"You know, it makes sense. She has been hanging around the local league for a while now. She reported on William's purchase of the team and maybe she felt some sort of loyalty with William and that's why she was so determined to undermine the Abington team. Either way, I'm glad you stopped by today. I meant to find you earlier, but you've been holed up in your office all day. Tonight, we're going to have a family meeting here at the ballpark. Your father and I want to go over the new roles and responsibilities that you have, and future opportunities as well. Are you able to get back here tonight?"

Madeline nodded.

"Good, we're meeting here in the conference room at seven. Now, I have to get back to some money-raising calls. We need to get some new sponsorships for the winter and beyond."

Madeline gave her mom a hug in appreciation for listening to her ramble on about the mess that she seemed to be in. Or at least the mess she was finding anyway.

She decided to take a quick turn around the ballpark before heading back to her desk for some more work emails before the end of the day. It was still relatively quiet with only the sounds of a few hitters in the outdoor batting cages and the sprinklers running in the outfield. Madeline walked over to the right field standing deck and looked down across the field. Breathing in the scent of the fresh cut grass and the lingering smell of peanuts that never seemed to go away, she thought about the past few weeks.

Losing her job, starting with the family business, stumbling over a dead body, her brother being a murder suspect, getting cleared, going on a date, reconnecting with Davis, and then the events of the previous night. It was almost too much to deal with. It had only been a month! She closed her eyes and took a few deep breaths. She heard a ding and rummaged in her pocket for her cell phone.

She had another text message from an unknown number. She knew that didn't bode well for the message. Clicking the application to open the text, she gasped. It was a message from Jennifer/Jessica.

Madeline, can we meet? I need to tell you some things. Meet me in the parking lot in two hours. — Jennifer Roberts

Before Madeline responded, she tried to think things through. So, this lady had connections it seemed with both the murder victim and the potential suspect in William Chase. Could she be dangerous? Madeline couldn't imagine that she would reach out if she had nefarious plans. She would know that Madeline would let Davis know. What other possible benefit did she have? Maybe she heard about William and wanted to clear the air about her relationship with William and the possible child they shared.

After deciding to meet with her that afternoon, she texted Davis to let him know what was going to happen. That way if something, god forbid, went wrong, someone would know what the plan was. She wasn't stupid. She wasn't going to walk into an unknown situation without a backup plan. Just in case. She hadn't talked to him since the incident in Barnstable the day before. She was hoping to see him in the office to debrief on what happened. He must've been elsewhere at the park that day because she still hadn't seen him. She wanted to pick his brain about the incident and also to smooth down the nervousness she was feeling about meeting up with Jennifer.

Madeline was not one who got gut feelings about things usually, but she definitely had a pit in her stomach when she thought about meeting up with her later. She wasn't sure how Jennifer fit into everything, but there was just something about the whole situation that made her uncomfortable. Well, she couldn't do anything at that point, she just had to wait and see what Jennifer wanted. The parking lot will hopefully still be full enough at that point in the days so there shouldn't be too much danger, if any. At least that's what she kept telling herself.

Chapter Twenty-Five

That afternoon, about an hour before she was going to meet with Jennifer, Madeline found herself fidgety and unable to focus. The whole murder thing was still weighing on her shoulders and now she was poised to hopefully get some answers. She just wanted to find out why and how everyone was connected and why Chris was murdered at the Abington ballpark. Why not anywhere else? It almost seemed like a direct attack on her family.

She tried to work on some emails and Facebook posts, but she couldn't keep her eyes from straying to the clock. She only had a quick text from Davis telling her that William was kept in the hospital overnight again for observation. The police apparently had questioned him once, but he didn't say much other than he didn't know who had hit him. He remembered having a meeting with her, and that the last thing he remembered that day was the receptionist leaving for home. Davis said he would be in the office the next day to catch up on things. She threw the phone down on her desk in frustration. She was hoping he'd be around to help her work this Jennifer thing.

So not much help there. She hoped the police knew that she didn't attack William. She had showed him the text luring her there, so it's not like she just showed up out of the blue. The police hadn't called her again to ask more questions, so that must have been a good sign she thought. She hoped that meant they had a better idea of who attacked him and knew that it wasn't Madeline.

Drumming her fingers on the desk, she glanced again at the clock for what seemed like the fifteenth time the past hour. She realized it was just about time to head to the parking lot. Madeline paused at Eliza's desk before she went out the door to let her know where she was going to be.

Eliza nodded at her and tapped the side of her nose. "I got you, girl. Make sure she tells you everything. If you're not back in an hour, I'll send out a search party." She gave Madeline a conspiratorial wink.

Madeline laughed as she made her way out the front entrance. She pulled up the recording app on her phone. She wanted to make sure she caught any confessions on tape. Of course, Jennifer was a pro, so Madeline didn't expect to get any information from her. Why would she want to talk to Madeline? Then again, she had thought the same thing about William and look how that turned out.

There were only a few cars left in the parking lot since it was after 5 p.m. on a non-game day. She wasn't sure what car she should be looking for. Of course, that news van from previous days was still parked in the back of the parking lot. Surely she wouldn't have driven that in, it seemed gaudy. The van had the news station emblazoned across the side and looked like some sort of conversion van changed into a news van.

As Madeline scoured the parking lot, she saw the van doors open and Jennifer's blonde head stuck out. Looking around, she gave Madeline a quick wave over and ducked back inside the van leaving one door propped open.

Shrugging, Madeline made her way through the parking lot to the van. By the time she got there, she had realized how quiet that part of the lot was. The van was parked at the very end of the lot in a corner spot lined by trees on one side. At that moment, she was really glad it was still light out. Seemed less threatening than if it was night out.

Brushing off a shiver of unease, Madeline approached the van. Jennifer was a news reporter, not some crazy person. She shouldn't be nervous. Madeline told herself to let Jennifer do all the talking and not to offer any information. She sidled up to the back door of the van, where one door was still propped open.

"Jennifer? Are you in there?" Madeline put her hand on the door frame and peered inside. She found several TV monitors and a large control board. What she didn't see was Jennifer. She heard a noise from the back of the van, closer to the cab. She knew from mystery novels and TV shows that she shouldn't proceed any further. Mysterious noises were nothing to play with. She wasn't crazy. Madeline backed away from the van door and felt a hand cover her mouth and another pull her arm behind her.

She tried to scream but the hand clutched her face tightly. A hoarse voice whispered in her ear. "Do not say anything or I will kill you. Just get in the van."

A hand pushed her into the interior of the van, and the door slammed before she could catch her breath and let out a scream. She felt the engine kick on and looked around for something to hold onto as she felt the vehicle move. Scanning the van, she couldn't find anything that might help her. No radio, no phone, no weapon of any kind. She scrounged in her back pocket for her cell phone and came up empty. It must have fallen out of her pocket when she was pushed in the car.

Crap. That was not ideal. At least she had remembered to tell Eliza what she was up to, and hopefully, she would check for her sooner rather than later. Madeline continued to scan the back of the van to see if there was something she could use to signal anyone. She saw a door leading to the front cab. Sliding across the floor of the van, she banged a fist against the door. She tried to pull it open, but it seemed to be locked from the other side.

"Jennifer? Is that you? What's going on? Where are you taking me? What's this all about?" Madeline tried to listen through the door, to see if she could hear any voices on the other side. The only noise was the engine. Putting her back against the door, she tried to gather her thoughts. Kidnapping now? This whole saga seemed so surreal.

She had just wanted to clear her brother's name. Why did all this drama have to happen now? And for real though, why was Jennifer so obsessed with her? She was just the social media consultant for her family baseball team. Not a police officer, not a detective. Madeline couldn't influence the police even if she wanted to. And yes, she'd been asking questions, but a murder happened at her place of business! Anyone would get themselves involved if that happened to them.

The car bounced over a set of train tracks, which made her wonder where Jennifer was taking her. If she had to guess, she thought they were heading towards Island Grove Park in Abington. The drive to the park from the stadium was only about five minutes, and there were two sets of tracks that they would have to go over if that's where they were heading. The park itself was pretty secluded, even though it was in the middle of town. There were two sides to park on, one in the woods and one along the lake.

Two minutes later, Madeline felt another bounce as they went over the second set of train tracks. She knew now that was where they were headed. She heard some sort of murmuring from the front seat. She couldn't tell if Jennifer was alone or if someone else was with her. Maybe she could take Jennifer when they stopped. As long as she was by herself, Madeline was confident she could overpower her.

Looking around the van again, she looked closer at the buttons on the control panel to see if any buttons could be pressed to draw attention to the van. She regretted not paying attention during school trips to the news station in high school. Maybe there was a button that could communicate with people on the outside. She just kept pressing buttons, but so far, she didn't have any luck. All the buttons had weird symbols on them, and of course there didn't seem to be any power in the back of the van either. She wasn't sure if that was typical of these types of media things. Not surprisingly, this was her first time in the back of a van.

She felt the van jerk to a halt and the engine cut off. She fell against the door that she had been leaning on as it opened behind her. Staring at her was Jennifer. Madeline guessed she should probably start thinking of her as Jessica from this point on. The surprise was when, from behind Jessica's shoulders, Ashley, Chris' old girlfriend, peered out.

"Ashley?" Madeline stared with her mouth open in shock. This was definitely something she wasn't expecting. She understood now that Jennifer/Jessica was a complete crackpot, but Ashley seemed genuinely devastated by Chris' death. Madeline had no idea she would be involved in all the mess. Ashley looked at her with tears in her eyes, but Madeline wasn't going to depend on her to help her out.

"Ashley!" Jessica snapped. "Snap out of it. We need to finish this now." Jessica pushed Madeline further back into the van and crawled through the opening to sit near her. "Okay, now you're going to tell me everything you know about the murder and what you think you know about the business. Otherwise, we're going to have issues." Her eyes glittered with menace. There was no doubt in Madeline's mind that she would hurt her if she had the chance.

Trying to buy time, Madeline spread her hands out. "Look, I don't know anything, truly. The only thing I know for sure is that you didn't go to high school with me. That's it! And as far as I know, that's not a crime."

Madeline heard the passenger door in the front clang open as Ashely exited the van. Madeline could only hope that Ashley would come to her senses and get some help for her. Madeline also hoped Eliza would remember to check on her and could summon help since she hadn't returned yet. She only wished she knew how long it would take. Madeline didn't trust Jessica not to hurt her. She had a crazy look in her eye, and now looked even crazier as she was held captive in the back of her van.

Chapter Twenty-Six

Jessica seemed to be getting more anxious with each passing minute. Madeline wanted to get her talking to give someone a chance to investigate why a news van was parked near Island Grove. The park itself wasn't that big, and locals used it as a fishing place all the time. It was surrounded by water on three sides, and further inside the park was an old Girl Scout campground and swimming hole. There were two parking areas, one in a residential neighborhood and one near the train tracks of the commuter rail into Boston. Jessica was smart—crazy, but smart. She probably parked on the side near the train tracks which was more isolated, shielding whatever her plan was from prying eyes.

They hadn't been gone from the Abington stadium for that long. Madeline knew the ride over must have only taken a few minutes. Even though there was no light let in from the back windows, she could see a sliver of sunlight through the door to the cab. Hopefully Jessica wouldn't try to hurt her in broad daylight. Then again, she did kidnap Madeline in broad daylight from her place of work, so who knows what she thought was a good idea.

"I told Chris not to get involved with your family. We had a good thing going with William, why involve more people if we didn't have to. Instead, he had to approach your brother and HAD to try and get him involved. The drugs were practically selling themselves and William was more than happy to help. Why did we need your family?" Jessica questioned while shaking her head.

Madeline saw that she was ranting at that point. She was content to let her talk, at least she knew that Jessica couldn't hurt her while she was talking. She didn't notice any weapons in Jessica's hand, but that didn't mean she couldn't clock her pretty hard. When she pushed Madeline in the van she felt pretty strong. Madeline on the other hand was pretty adverse to most exercise and probably not in shape enough to fight anyone off. She just had to keep her talking and hope that someone would come along or Ashley would get a backbone and decide to help her. One could hope. She didn't seem like the strongest person mentally. If they could get out of the van, then maybe Madeline would have a fighting chance.

Jessica was still talking while Madeline was pondering her options. "After all Chris and I did to set up this venture and William wanted to back out, and then Chris had to go and get involved with your brother. It's not like we planned at all. We were supposed to stay small. Focus on making money by selling the drugs to the kids playing for the Barnstable team. William was only too willing to help me since I am the mother of his daughter. I could keep that kid away from him for years if he didn't cooperate. Then, he got a conscience and was going to spill all to you. Of course I couldn't let that happen."

Looking at her in horror, Madeline said, "So you leveraged your child to sell drugs? And murder your own boyfriend?" Her head snapped up and her eyes bored into Madeline's.

She let out a brittle laugh. "Boyfriend? Chris wasn't my boyfriend. He was my brother. We weren't raised together; in fact, I didn't even know about him until after I hooked up with William. Oh, don't look at me like that. We all do what we have to do in this world to get by. My brother wasn't a good guy. The world is better off without him. Now, I just have to deal with you, too." She got a manic look in her eyes. "After I take care of you, I'll move somewhere completely different and change my life. No one would ever think that the mild-mannered TV reporter would be involved in a murder."

Jessica began to rummage around a small black duffel bag she had grabbed from the front seat. Pulling a roll of duct tape out, she started tearing strips off. While she did that, Madeline could've sworn that she heard another car pull into the parking lot. Jessica seemed too distracted to notice. Madeline wondered why Ashley didn't raise the alarm for her partner, but before she could do anything, Jessica lurched across the van and taped Madeline's mouth shut. Taking two more strips, she then bound Madeline's hands in front of her and then taped her feet together, too.

Her options for escape were dwindling fast.

"Now, Maddie, I can call you Maddie, right? Not that it matters. I'm going to be right back and we're going to take a walk to the lake. So stay where you are." She laughed manically, looking at Madeline bound in front of her. She opened the door to the cab and shoved Madeline headfirst into the front two seats and shut the door behind her tightly.

Frantic, Madeline kicked her legs and pressed buttons along the radio with her hands and feet, hoping that one of them would alert people nearby. She must have kicked the headlight lever because the lights bounced off the trees in front of the van. Using her taped feet, she slammed her feet on the steering wheel hoping to get to the horn. Finally, she hit it in just the right place and the horn blared loudly through the quiet park.

Suddenly, Madeline heard a thud against the side of the van. After a chaotic few seconds, the passenger side door opened, and she saw Detective Stephenson standing there with Jessica in handcuffs. He looked at her shocked, as her head was upside down on the passenger seat and her legs were hanging on the steering wheel column.

The detective handed off Jessica to a patrolman and helped Madeline untangle herself from the cab of the van. She saw Davis and Eliza standing near the squad car that was taking custody of Jessica. She was swearing and yelling every name in the book at the young officer as he pushed her head down into the waiting cruiser. Madeline wasn't close enough to hear everything, but she imagined that the police officer was hoping that Jessica would exercise her right to remain silent as soon as possible.

Breaking through the crowd of police, Eliza came running up to Madeline and threw her arms around her neck. Unfortunately, Madeline was still taped at the hands and her mouth so all she could do was let out a muffled yelp. Davis appeared next to Eliza holding a Swiss army knife. Cutting the tape off her hands and gently easing the tape off her mouth, he squeezed her arm with a look of concern in his eyes. Madeline smiled gratefully at him and looked around at the chaos.

"How did you guys know where I was?" She asked both of her friends.

"Well, I got a bad feeling when you left to go meet her outside. So, I paged Davis on the walkie and he went into the parking lot with me to find out. She must've just taken you because your cell phone was lying on the ground." Eliza said with tears in her eyes. "We called the police right away and I told them about the missing news van from that part of the parking lot. The police spotted the van in the Island Grove parking lot and Detective Stephenson brought us over."

"Well, Eliza, am I ever glad for your intuition. Jennifer or Jessica or whatever was behind everything. Apparently, they had some sort of steroid ring running and were blackmailing William to participate. She is the mother of his daughter and was planning to skip town." Taking a deep breath, Madeline tried to calm her racing heartbeat. It was just starting to sink in to her about how dangerous the situation was and how close she was to being seriously hurt or worse.

Davis looked at her with concern. "Are you sure you're okay? Do you want to head to the hospital to get checked out?"

Madeline shook her head. Luckily, she didn't feel too injured. The most Jessica did to her was push her hard into the van. No lasting injures. Other than the psychological effects of being kidnapped by a crazy murderous news reporter. That would probably be something she would need to work through later when things calmed down. "I think I just want to let my parents know everything is okay and it's finally over."

Madeline knew she couldn't leave right away. The police needed her statement. Detective Stephenson let Davis drive Madeline over to the police station which luckily wasn't too far away. She met the detective in a small conference room. Handing her a cup of tea, he sat down in front of her with a tape recorder. "Are you ready to give your statement?"

Madeline nodded and the detective pressed the small button on the old school tape recorder. She wondered if the town knew you could record conversations with cell phones now. Somehow, she didn't think it would be an appropriate time for that conversation.

She took a deep breath and began with finding the picture of William's daughter at his office when he was injured. That led to her investigating Jennifer and finding that she was actually Jessica Jenkins. That dovetailed into finding how she was connected to Chris Dailey. She didn't think there was anything serious about it, but now she realized that William was going to confess to her when he got injured. That must have been why he was so adamant to meet her in the past few weeks.

Detective Stephenson looked across the table at her and shook his head. "Madeline, we're glad you're okay. We were actually looking for Jessica when we got the call about you being taken. William Chase woke up this morning and told us everything. He gave up the whole steroid scheme with Jessica and Chris. How his child was being leveraged for cooperation in the ring. Even the murder of Chris by Jessica. Jennifer. She apparently had taken the keys from one of the cleaning crew at the park and arranged to meet Chris in the dugout. She hoped that it was the type of location that couldn't connect to either of them. When he tried to back out of their deal, she took a bat from the visitor bin and bashed him over the head. Then she got Ashley involved. When Jennifer, or Jessica, kidnapped you today, Ashley knew things were serious. Even though we had a general idea what happened, Ashley helped fill in some of the blanks when we picked her up at the van."

Madeline shuddered. She couldn't believe Jessica would murder her own brother. She didn't even seem to have remorse when she talked about it in the van.

It was almost clinical the way she talked about the steroid ring and both William and Chris.

"We have enough evidence against her now with William's testimony to charge her with murder, and of course with her kidnapping you as well. We are really glad you're okay. You have some good, smart friends there who know how to take care of you. The police will be in contact with you to get some more information." He stood up and turned to leave the room. As he reached the door, he turned around one more time. "But maybe lay off the investigations for a while. Not that we don't appreciate what you found out, but maybe next time leave the police work to the actual police, okay?"

Madeline gave him a salute and smile. No worries there. She could put this whole thing behind her and get back to the baseball season. She definitely didn't want any more drama in her life. She had enough to last her for weeks. She took one more cleansing breath before leaving the conference room. Davis was sitting in the waiting room looking at his phone. He must've heard her come out because he looked up and jumped out of his chair.

"Ready to go? I'll give you a ride. Your car can stay at the ballpark tonight and I'll drive you to work in the morning. Is that okay?" He guided her out to his car. His hand on the small of her back felt so comforting, she didn't want him to move it.

"Thanks, Davis. I appreciate your help. I don't know what would've happened if you and Eliza didn't think to come looking for me." Madeline brushed a tear off her cheek. Uh-oh, things were probably starting to hit her.

They pulled up in front of her house and Davis turned to look at her. He seemed to be looking for something to say. She didn't want to break the spell in the car. It was so comfortable and safe that she wanted to stay in that moment forever.

Finally, he sighed. "Maddie, I'm really so glad you're okay. When Eliza first told me what you were going to do, I freaked out. I mean, I knew you were questioning things, but I never thought that it would go this far." He looked out the front window and cleared his throat. "I don't know if this is inappropriate or not, seeing as you are sort of my boss, but I want to take you out sometime. Outside of the office, I mean. Like a date."

Her heart beat fast in her chest. All her high school dreams were coming true. He wanted to take her on a date. If she hadn't been tied up in a van a few hours ago, she probably would've jumped him right then and there.

Instead, she smiled at him. "I would love that."

Breaking into a relieved smile, he nodded. "Great. I have tickets to the Sox game next week. We can do dinner beforehand. Now, I'm going to wait until you're locked up inside. I know the bad guys have been caught, but I just want to make sure you're safe. You are okay, right?"

Madeline assured him she was fine. She just wanted to go inside, snuggle with the cats, and have the largest glass of wine she could find to try and forget the afternoon. He sat in his car as she scrambled out and pulled her keys from her purse. Luckily, Eliza had put her purse in the car when they heard she was found. She didn't want to have to go back to the ballpark to pick anything up after the police station. She needed time to process everything that happened.

Chapter Twenty-Seven

The next day, Madeline slept through her alarm for the first time in forever. She surmised that the pint glass of wine she had the night before had a large effect on her sleeping in the next morning. Every muscle ached, and she still felt the red welts on her wrists from where Jessica had taped them. She reached over to her nightstand, knocking one of the cats in the head and looked at her phone. It was 9 a.m., and she knew she should probably get up and call Davis for a ride to the ballpark.

Stretching, she sniffed and found the aroma of bacon wafting down the hallway from her kitchen. She heard humming and realized her mom was in the kitchen. She pulled on an oversized college sweatshirt and stumbled down the hallway, rubbing her eyes.

"Good morning." Her mom turned around at the sound of her voice and dropped the spatula she had been holding. Pulling Madeline into a big hug, she squeezed until Madeline couldn't breathe. "Mom, I'm really okay."

"Oh, sweetie. Davis called and told us everything as soon as you had been taken. Eliza then told us the rest while you were at the police station. She let us know you were okay and in good health. I used my key this morning to let myself in. I didn't think you'd be going into the office early like you always do."

She picked up the spatula and flipped over the pancakes on the griddle. They were Madeline's favorite kind, chocolate chip. Perfect recovery food.

"Thanks, Mom. I'm glad you're here. I'm just so glad everything is over." The cats trotted into the room and started winding themselves around her legs. She went over to the small pantry and filled up two bowls of cat food. All three cats immediately left her side to gobble down food. Cats were such fickle creatures.

Pulling up a chair to her kitchen island, she sat with her chin resting on her hand. Thinking of all the events from the day before, she still couldn't quite believe that Jennifer Roberts, the reporter, was really Jessica and responsible for a murder. It was crazy. "Mom, did you know that William Chase had a secret life?"

She placed a large stack of pancakes in front of Madeline. Turning off the stove burners, she came and sat down, too. "You know, we never really had that much information about him to begin with when he bought the Barnstable team. Usually the other teams like to get together with the new owners of teams as a sort of welcoming committee. We never got the chance with William. He was very secretive and ran his team like a major league organization. I guess it's not that surprising that he had a whole other side of him."

"What do you think is going to happen to his team now? I can't imagine he's going to get away with being part of the steroid ring," Madeline said.

Her mother looked thoughtful. "I honestly don't know. The team itself will probably undergo massive drug testing, and then, with the results of that, they might be suspended for the rest of the season. In regards to actual ownership of the team, who knows?"

She poured another cup of coffee and handed Madeline an iced tea to wash down the breakfast. "Now, are you up to coming to the field today? We have some announcements to make that we wanted to do last night before things got crazy. I just want to make sure you feel up to it."

Madeline thought for a minute. She thought going to the park might be helpful. Better than sitting at home thinking about everything. "Of course, let me run upstairs and shower. Give me twenty minutes and I'll be ready."

Shooing her away with her hands, her mother went about cleaning up the dishes. Madeline loved when her mom took care of her, it brought back such good memories. Dashing to the shower, she hopped in. After a quick shower, she changed into jeans and a team shirt. Pulling her hair back in a headband she headed back to the living room in just about fifteen minutes.

On the way to the ballpark in her mom's care, they listened to some Top 40 radio station that her Mom loved. She loved being the person who heard new music first. It was adorable. By the time they arrived at the field, they were both singing along to some new song they heard. It made her mom feel like one of the cool kids.

Laughing, they got out of the car and headed to the front entrance arm in arm. The field was being worked on for the game that weekend. When they walked into the front office, Madeline saw a crush of people standing around Eliza's desk. At the sound of the door opening, everyone turned around and rushed around her at one time, shaking her hand, giving her hugs, and generally asking if she was okay.

Her brother and dad were at the back of the receiving crush and she gave them both big hugs. Choking back tears, her father cleared his throat. "I'm so glad you're safe, sweetie. I can't believe everything that happened. Thank goodness you made it out safely."

"The real thanks belong to Eliza and Davis for raising the alarm. They were the real heroes in this crazy situation." Madeline pulled Eliza into a hug.

"Well," her father cleared his throat to get everyone's attention. "Now that everyone is here, I have a few announcements to make." He made his way to the front of the crowd. "As you know, this has been a crazy few weeks. Well, in the ensuing events, we got a piece of great news. Ben will be leaving us to join the front office of the Red Sox officially at the end of this current season."

Madeline clapped her hands until they hurt and felt her eyes well up in pride. She was so happy for Ben. It was always the dream to work for the majors. She was so glad he could get the opportunity especially after all the murder stuff of the past few weeks. She gave her brother a big smile and squeezed his hand.

Her father held his hands up to quiet the clapping. Everyone turned their attention back to her parents. "To that end, we would also like to announce that Madeline will now step into her brother's role at the end of the season to work higher up in our front office. We hope one day she will be in charge of the whole thing."

Madeline's jaw dropped open. She couldn't believe that it was happening. Her mom did float the idea before, but she didn't think it would happen that soon. Granted, they still had three more months left in the season, so it's not like she'd be running things tomorrow. She felt a nervous excitement. She couldn't remember ever feeling like that at other jobs. This could be the start of something great. And to top it off, she had a date with Davis. She looked over and found him smiling at her. She smiled back. Yeah, this just might work out after all.

The End

Acknowledgments

This is my moment! I always imagined my acknowledgement section of my book to be like my acceptance speech for when I won a Grammy. Cause I was going to win one at some point.

First and foremost, I want to thank my parents. My mom, Nancy Asselin, for being my best friend and sounding board. She puts up with me and doesn't judge me too harshly. Well, she judges me as a mom should judge her children, and she tries to keep me accountable for things. She is the literal best, and I wouldn't be where I am without her! To my dad, Robert Asselin, who has been my champion since the time he celebrated my first birthday deployed in a submarine, having a cake with his shipmates. He has supported me through dance classes, college, and now adulthood, and I wouldn't be where I am without his support either!

To my little brother, Brandon Asselin. You kept me on my toes when we were younger, but I'm glad we're adults now and can be friends.

Thanks to Pandamoon Publishing for taking on my dream book! Red Sox fans know no boundaries and I'm glad we found each other. Thanks to Jess Reino for being an AMAZING editor (and fellow Masshole).

To my English teachers through the years, from Mr. Kirkpatrick in 9th grade at Cumberland Valley HS, to Dr. Hunter at Curry College. They instilled in me a love of reading, a love of the classics, and a love of writing.

To my Sisters in Crime (NE and National) who have answered my questions, supported my work, and given me opportunities to network with other authors. It is the best community I have ever been a part of hands down.

To all the friends that have listened to me talk about this book and still wanted to hang out with me, you guys are the best. To my "girls" from that job that shall remain nameless, I miss our happy hours and trips to Sullivan's in the summah!

To my bestie, Mary Borgendale, thank you for being a friend (Golden Girls FTW!). Sassy pants Kara and little CJ have a great mother and I'm glad to call you my friend. Special thanks to Shelly Dickson Carr, who I met at my very first Malice Domestic conference and got me thinking about what kind of book I would want to write. It inspired me to write the baseball-themed mystery I always wanted.

And yes, I'm going to thank my cats. Cause they're my babies and I love them (Julia, Jacques, and Madeline). To anyone and everyone else in my life, just know you have all had a profound impact on me and I appreciate all of you for supporting me on this journey!

And special thanks to the Boston Red Sox. I love you and I love our World Series memories. Special shout out to Dustin Pedroia….my Grandpa met him once and from then on spoke of "his best friend, Pedroia."

About the Author

Nicole Asselin grew up a Navy Brat, moving around with her family and her Naval Officer father as he was stationed in various U.S. locales including Monterey, CA and Honolulu, HI. She spent her formative high school years in the middle of Pennsylvania, but always identified with her New England roots. Her family is originally from New England and she always loved the weather in the north. Nicole graduated from Curry College in Milton, Mass with a degree in English/Creative Writing, minoring in Dance in 2004.

As she tried to decide what to do with her life, she attended George Mason University and received a Master's in Arts Management, which of course was then parlayed into a job as a "jack-of-all trades" technical writer in the Government Contracting world. She worked in that sector for over ten years before transitioning to a new field.

Now working just outside of Boston at a healthcare company as a Technical Writer, she lives on the South Shore of Massachusetts with her three cats Julia, Jacques, and Madeline (no relation to the main character of her book).

Nicole's family is originally from Connecticut. Her Grandpa Asselin introduced her into the Red Sox nation where she has been a member for her whole life and her Grandma Asselin introduced her to the world of mystery novels. Now those two loves are combined into her new Ballpark Mystery Series.

Nicole is a current member of Sisters in Crime (National and New England) and the Mystery Writers of America. She sits on the Board of Directors for the NE branches of both groups as Social Media Liaison. She's attended several conferences in the past few years to study the craft including Malice Domestic, Bouchercon, and the NE Crime Bake. All the classes and conferences have helped groom her novel into "Murder at First Pitch."

Her short story, "Mile High Murder" can be found as part of Z Publishing's "America's Emerging Suspense Writers: East Region" published in early 2019.

Thank you for purchasing this copy of *Murder at First Pitch*. If you enjoyed this book, please let the author know by posting a review.

pandamoon
publishing

Growing good ideas into great reads…one book at a time.

Visit http://www.pandamoonpublishing.com to learn about other works by our talented authors.

Mystery/Thriller/Suspense

Science Fiction/Fantasy

- *Children of Colonodona Book 1: The Wizard's Apprentice* by Alisse Lee Goldenberg
- *Children of Colonodona Book 2: The Island of Mystics* by Alisse Lee Goldenberg
- *Dybbuk Scrolls Trilogy Book 1: The Song of Hadariah* by Alisse Lee Goldenberg
- *Dybbuk Scrolls Trilogy Book 2: The Song of Vengeance* by Alisse Lee Goldenberg
- *Dybbuk Scrolls Trilogy Book 3: The Song of War* by Alisse Lee Goldenberg
- *Everly Series Book 1: Everly* by Meg Bonney
- *.EXE Chronicles Book 1: Hello World* by Alexandra Tauber and Tiffany Rose
- *Finder Series Book 1: Chimera Catalyst* by Susan Kuchinskas
- *Fried Windows (In a Light White Sauce)* by Elgon Williams
- *Magehunter Saga Book 1: Magehunter* by Jeff Messick
- *Revengers Series Book 1: Revengers* by David Valdes Greenwood
- *The Bath Salts Journals: Volume One* by Alisse Lee Goldenberg and An Tran
- *The Crimson Chronicles Book 1: Crimson Forest* by Christine Gabriel
- *The Crimson Chronicles Book 2: Crimson Moon* by Christine Gabriel
- *The Phaethon Series Book 1: Phaethon* by Rachel Sharp
- *The Sitnalta Series Book 1: Sitnalta* by Alisse Lee Goldenberg
- *The Sitnalta Series Book 2: The Kingdom Thief* by Alisse Lee Goldenberg
- *The Sitnalta Series Book 3: The City of Arches* by Alisse Lee Goldenberg
- *The Sitnalta Series Book 4: The Hedgewitch's Charm* by Alisse Lee Goldenberg
- *The Sitnalta Series Book 5: The False Princess* by Alisse Lee Goldenberg
- *The Thuperman Trilogy Book 1: Becoming Thuperman* by Elgon Williams
- *The Thuperman Trilogy Book 2: Homer Underby* by Elgon Williams
- *The Wolfcat Chronicles Book 1: Wolfcat 1* by Elgon Williams

Women's Fiction

- *Beautiful Secret* by Dana Faletti
- *The Long Way Home* by Regina West
- *The Mason Siblings Series Book 1: Love's Misadventure* by Cheri Champagne
- *The Mason Siblings Series Book 2: The Trouble with Love* by Cheri Champagne
- *The Mason Siblings Series Book 3: Love and Deceit* by Cheri Champagne
- *The Mason Siblings Series Book 4: Final Battle for Love* by Cheri Champagne
- *The Seductive Spies Series Book 1: The Thespian Spy* by Cheri Champagne
- *The Seductive Spy Series Book 2: The Seamstress and the Spy* by Cheri Champagne
- *The Shape of the Atmosphere* by Jessica Dainty
- *The To-Hell-And-Back Club Book 1: The To-Hell-And-Back Club* by Jill Hannah Anderson
- *The To-Hell-And-Back Club Book 2: Crazy Little Town Called Love* by Jill Hannah Anderson

Made in the USA
Coppell, TX
21 February 2023

13205895R00105